THE A-LIST
HOLLYWOOD ROYALTY

A-LIST NOVELS BY ZOEY DEAN:

THE A-LIST

GIRLS ON FILM

BLONDE AMBITION

TALL COOL ONE

BACK IN BLACK

SOME LIKE IT HOT

AMERICAN BEAUTY

HEART OF GLASS

BEAUTIFUL STRANGER

CALIFORNIA DREAMING

HOLLYWOOD ROYALTY

If you like THE A-LIST, you may also enjoy:

The **Poseur** series by Rachel Maude
The **Secrets of My Hollywood Life** series by Jen Calonita
Footfree and Fancyloose by Elizabeth Craft and Sarah Fain
Haters by Alisa Valdes-Rodriguez
Betwixt by Tara Bray Smith

THE A-LIST
HOLLYWOOD ROYALTY

ZOEY DEAN

poppy

LITTLE, BROWN AND COMPANY
New York   Boston

Poppy

Little, Brown and Company
Hachette Book Group
237 Park Avenue, New York, NY 10017
For more of your favorite series, go to www.pickapoppy.com

First Edition: January 2009

Poppy is an imprint of Little, Brown Books for Young Readers.
The Poppy name and logo are trademarks of Hachette Book Group, Inc.

alloyentertainment
Produced by Alloy Entertainment
151 West 26th Street, New York, NY 10001

Cover design by Andrea C. Uva
Cover model photography by Roger Moenks
Cover background photography by Andrea C. Uva

ISBN-978-0-316-03181-3

10 9 8 7 6 5 4 3 2 1
CWO
Printed in the United States of America

For Steve, my partner in everything from crime to comedy.

Let's face it: I want it all—just like you and everybody else. It may not be in the cards, but the prospect is so dazzling that I have to try.

—Lauren Bacall

FAIRY PRUDENESS

Even before the white stretch limo pulled to a stop outside the Nokia Theatre, Amelie Adams could hear the screams of hundreds of fans. She blinked out the tinted windows as the driver slowed to a stop in front of the ruby red carpet. Behind the ground-level throngs of fans and photographers, models stood on six-foot risers, wearing hot pink Prada sunglasses and bright white tent dresses with graphic prints of L.A. landmarks on them: the Hollywood sign, Grauman's Chinese, the Beverly Hills Hotel, a postcard shot of Malibu. Most of the fans barely paid attention to the glamazons; they were more interested in catching a glimpse of their favorite Hollywood starlets arriving for the premiere of *The A-List*.

"Fairy Princess!"

"Fairy Princess!"

Even though Amelie wasn't in the movie, her fans knew she was coming tonight. Clusters of little girls waved homemade, glittery signs proclaiming their high-pitched love for her Kidz Network character, Fairy Princess. Amelie leaned back in her seat, pushing a red ringlet from her turquoise eyes.

Across from Amelie, her mother's face broke into the wide, voluptuous smile that Amelie had inherited. Helen Adams's own red hair was shorter—shaped into a face-framing chin-length bob by Mario, her one-name-only personal hairdresser for the last ten years—and her eyes were a dark hazel, but otherwise she and Amelie could have been mistaken for sisters.

"Have fun. And remember, you'll get it next time." She winked one heavily mascaraed eye and smoothed her strapless violet Carolina Herrera gown over a flat stomach courtesy of a three-week fitness boot camp in Studio City.

Amelie's gloss-lacquered lips formed a grimace. She'd been up for the part of Emma Hardy, *The A-List*'s lead, but had lost the role to Marlee Aces, a blonde with one screen credit in a sexy indie, *Rock My World*—about a lesbian heavy metal band in Mormon Utah. The producers had deemed her "more mature" and therefore better for the part. The Emma character had a sex scene, and while Amelie knew that a jump from petting winged ponies to heavy petting would've been a risky career move, sometimes she longed to do *something* that wasn't G-rated.

"No scowls." Helen leaned over to kiss her daughter on the cheek. "And have fun. I'm going to take a quick meeting about your Christmas special, but I'll find you at the party later."

Amelie reached back, giving her mom's hand a squeeze, as two tuxedoed valets reached in to extract her from the limo.

"Fairy Princess! Fairy Princess!"

Amelie stepped out of the limousine, plastering on the same magical grin that had sold four million T-shirts with her face on them. Her new white patent Miu Miu wedges sank into the plush carpet and she gracefully adjusted the hem of her silver Jovani flapper-inspired dress. Her character wore pink *exclusively*, so it was nice to not feel like human cotton candy for once.

She made her way down the row of crazed fans—the younger ones near tears—signing glossy pictures, massive posters, and *BOP* magazines in her trademark swirly script. After each autograph, she flourished her pink Sharpie with Fairy Princess's signature wand wave. *Elbow left, wrist swish, elbow right, wrist swish.*

At the far end of the red carpet, cast members from *The A-List* mingled with other actors about her age. Raven-haired Kady Parker and milky-skinned Moira and Deven Lacey, twins whose trademark sexy scowls had helped them get parts on *School of Scandal*, a new CW show, shot her curious glances and then returned to their conversation.

Used to being ignored by her Hollywood peers, Amelie sighed, signing a talking Fairy Princess doll with bubble gum pink hair and glittery accessories. She knew she was lucky to be seated at the helm of a multimillion-dollar empire at only sixteen, but sometimes she just wanted to move up from the kids' table. She was growing up, but no one besides Mary Ellen, the on-set stylist who'd had to let her Fairy Princess wardrobe out in the chest, had really seemed to notice.

Amelie smiled at a white-blond seven-year-old in a replica of Fairy Princess's Winter Festival ball gown. She held up a shirt for Amelie to sign. "Is it true you're playing a new kind of fairy in *Class Angel*?" the little girl asked, awestruck.

"You got it," Amelie answered, shooting another dazzling smile that almost outshone her dress's sequins and crystals. Filming started on her new movie, *Class Angel*, the day after tomorrow. It was PG, and more mature than her Fairy Princess role, but she still played a teenager's guardian angel rather than an *actual* teenager. It was like calling Pinkberry ice cream.

Amelie leaned over the metal barricade railing to sign the shirt, her face inches from the little girl's.

"Mommy!" The little girl pointed at Amelie, then yelled, "Mom, Fairy Princess has boobies!"

Amelie felt the blood rush to her face. Well, then. Maybe people *were* noticing her growing up, after all. . . .

Amelie stood bathed in the sapphire-blue lights cast by the Nokia's looming facade. She'd barely paid attention to the ninety-minute movie, mentally replaying her red carpet humiliation instead of focusing on the film. Not that she could have focused even if she'd tried. She'd given up her primo reserved seat to an agent who'd brought his grandmother, and had wound up seated next to three fifteen-year-old girls who'd driven in from the Inland Empire after winning tickets on KROQ. They'd snuck in cans of Coors Light with them, and Amelie had struggled to hear the movie over their giggly conversation about the cute slacker who'd sold them the beer at 7-Eleven. She stretched her tired neck from side to side, wishing she could skip the afterparty and head home. Unfortunately, she knew she had to put in an appearance, or her absence would be chalked up to sour grapes.

Now she stood just outside the outdoor party area,

watching people trickle out from the theater. Stars donned their occasionally misguided interpretations of the invite-specified "sexy *A-List* evening wear": skin-baring miniskirts, long glittery gowns that looked like expensive prom dresses. Security was already manning the makeshift entrance to the afterparty area, to make sure that people like Amelie's drunken underage seat-mates didn't crash.

She'd do one turn around the party space, meet and greet with some studio bigwigs, smile big, look sweet, and get the heck out of there. Amelie had an early call time tomorrow to shoot a music video for the Kidz Network site, anyway. It was the perfect excuse to trade her painful wedges for her Paul Frank monkey slippers. Add a bowl of Häagen-Dazs and her *Veronica Mars* DVDs, and she was set for the evening.

Someone tapped her on the back. "Hey, do you mind walking in with me?"

Amelie turned. Kady Parker was standing by herself, her wide sapphire blue eyes shimmering beneath the fringe of glossy black bangs that framed her heart-shaped face. "I always feel weird walking into a party alone."

Kady Parker was her costar in *Class Angel*. Since getting into the business as a twelve-year-old, Kady almost always played the sassy tomboy who gets kicked around by bitchy prom queen types but gets the guy in the end. Amelie nodded, half surprised that Kady—whom she'd met only briefly, at a table read—was being so friendly.

"Cool," Kady said, flashing her wristband and leading the way. The movie premiere might have been open to the hundredth caller, but the afterparty was strictly by invitation only, and you needed a "Get *A*-ed" wristband, which of course they both had. "Hot dress, by the way."

"You look great too," Amelie replied. Kady's feminine-cut black Armani tux fit her slightly rebellious movie persona and her petite frame.

"Thanks. Let's hit the bar—you can meet some of the other girls from *Class Angel*," Kady half-shouted over the new Santogold song, leading Amelie into a courtyard area, where four bars were set up in a square. The platform models now wore opaque white Prada one-piece swimsuits and the kind of sultry yet bored expressions mastered only through lots of practice. They danced languidly to the music as guests loaded their plates with food from the catered buffet. Three twentysomething brunettes hovered at a cocktail table, congratulating themselves for getting in without wristbands.

Kady paused, standing on the tiptoes of her already-high cherry red Christian Louboutin stilettos, searching the crowd for her friends. "I don't know what they'll be drinking tonight," she said.

The four bars were all serving drinks inspired by the characters, and behind each was a backdrop featuring a glamorous publicity shot of one of the *A-List* actors. The Emma bar was serving classic cocktails like Manhattans and martinis, and rare Opus One wine in an exclusive *A-List* vintage. A bar for Peter, Emma's on-and-off-again love interest, was serving twenty microbrewed beers in frosted glasses. The bar for Sarah, a super-rich character with movie star parents (allegedly based on young director Sam Sharpe), offered Cristal, Veuve, and Dom Pérignon champagnes, while a bar for Dahlia, the wild child with a mean streak, served potent vodka, rum, and tequila combos.

"There they are," Kady said, grabbing Amelie's arm and leading her to the Dahlia bar. A group of bored-looking girls stood around a shiny silver cocktail table. The Lacey twins slouched on stools, sipping identical Grey Goose and cranberry cocktails. They were mirror images of each other, with endlessly toned legs, thick caramel hair, and the same "don't mess with us" expressions. (Though rumor had it that three-minutes-younger Deven was actually a sweetheart.) Next to them stood DeAndra Barnett, a former child model who'd made her foray into acting in the massive Kidz Network hit *West High Story*. She had luminous toffee-colored skin, a lean, athletic body, and short curly hair that highlighted her sharp cheekbones. She wore a strapless D&G dress in a wild lily-and-leopard print that kept falling down her skinny chest.

"You guys know Amelie, right?" Kady gestured to Amelie as though she were a showcase prize on *The Price Is Right*.

DeAndra squinted as though she barely recognized Amelie, gracelessly pulling up her dress. The twins smiled faintly. "*Fairy Princess*, right?" they said in unison. Amelie nodded.

"*Fairy Princess*, and *Class Angel* with me and DeAndra," Kady corrected. "And now Hunter, too."

Hunter?

Amelie thought she was hearing things. Kady could only be talking about one Hunter. Hunter Sparks. The guy so hot his role in *West High Story* had propelled little girls from their "I hate boys" phases directly into their "I heart Hunter" obsessions.

"Wait, Hunter Sparks is in *Class Angel*?" Amelie

fought to sound casual as her brain hyperventilated: *HunterSparksHunterSparksHunterSparks!*

Amelie had starred in her first feature with him, when she was eleven and he was fourteen, before her Fairy Princess reign began. He played her older brother, who died trying to save Amelie when aliens invaded Chicago. Even though he treated her in a brother-sister way the whole shoot, she'd fallen totally in love with him. She still had script pages covered in hearts filled with loopy cursive musings: "I love Hunter," "Mrs. Hunter Sparks," and "Mrs. Amelie Adams-Sparks." For five years, she'd barely run into him, even at Kidz Network headquarters. And, yet, just glimpsing his face on a *West High Story* poster or hearing his name was enough to make her heart thud in double time, the way it did now.

"I thought our lead was Raleigh Springfield," Amelie hastily added, naming the actor who was originally slated to play the role.

"Nope, he's out." Kady shrugged. "Said he wants to do an indie instead, but I think it's just rehab. The producer called in a favor and Hunter's in."

"Cool." The twins nodded and drained their glasses. "He's yummier anyway. Raleigh has that greasy hair."

A delightful tingle worked its way through Amelie's body. Her stars were falling into place, *Fairy Princess* style.

"Anyway, this party blows, K." The twins looked at Kady like two dogs begging their owner to take them outside.

"Okay, then," Kady said, processing the info. "We could hit the Standard, the downtown one on Flower." She turned to Amelie. "Have you been? The rooftop bar has waterbed pods and great bottle service. And no wannabes." She glanced at the uninvited brunettes in Payless heels at one of the bars.

Before Amelie could answer, she felt a hand on her shoulder.

"Hi girls." Amelie's mom's voice strained over the noise. Amelie flushed with embarrassment. "Amelie, honey, they moved up the call time for tomorrow by a few hours. The limo's waiting out front."

Amelie turned back to Kady, who'd probably never brought her mom to a premiere before. She shrugged. "Thanks for the invite, but it looks like I've got to call it a night."

She made an apologetic face, though secretly she was thankful for the interruption. Party hopping was fine if you wanted to end up with a has-been rep and a drug habit by age twenty-one on *E! True Hollywood Story*, but Amelie intended to be the industry's anti-Lohan, thank you very much.

"No worries," Kady said, hugging Amelie. "I'll see you on Sunday."

"For sure," Amelie said, waving at the other girls as she grabbed her clutch off the cocktail table.

Helen led the way back through the crowd, walking with her perfect Pilates posture. "They seemed nice. You might have fun on this movie."

Amelie grinned. She and Kady didn't have to get matching BFF bracelets, but at least Kady didn't seem like the kind of crazy costar who'd put Nair in Amelie's shampoo bottle. Plus, a movie where she didn't have to match dance steps with whimsical sprites? One that might even have Hunter Sparks?

Amelie was definitely ready for her close-up.

DELAYED GRATIFICATION

Myla Everhart stood in the LAX baggage claim, wishing she hadn't worn her thigh-high, yellow Aztec-print Pucci Sundial dress—every time she sat down, the back of her legs touched some invariably sticky surface.

The first daughter of America's hottest on- and off-screen couple craned her neck, looking toward the doors to the street. Ash had said he'd park and come inside to help shield her from the paparazzi and carry her bags. Granted, she'd internationally overnighted everything via Luggage Concierge, but he could certainly carry her plum Marc Jacobs tote full of French *Vogues* and her cashmere travel blanket.

Myla fished her emerald-adorned iPhone from the bottom of her bag. One fourteen. Ash knew she landed at twelve thirty. What was the freaking holdup?

But then . . . that was Ash. Her Ash. Laid-back, easygoing Ash.

She softened, just thinking of him. Long before they'd gotten together, Ash Gilmour had been her best friend and the only guy who *got* Myla. It wasn't easy going through puberty as the child of Barkley Everhart and

Lailah Barton—*People*'s Most Beautiful Couple, 2001, 2002, 2006–present. Most Inattentive, too, by Myla's standards. They'd adopted Myla as a baby after spending time on-set in Thailand, filming an Adam and Eve–inspired love story that had grossed some ungodly amount. It had been just Myla, until four years ago, when they'd brought home four-year-old Mahalo from Bangladesh on her twelfth birthday. They'd just returned from a *Babel*-meets–*Independence Day* shoot and decided to bring back a souvenir. At least that's how it seemed to Myla.

Then one day in the eighth grade, she and Ash were waiting for his dad, Gordon Gilmour—a record producer who spent more time coddling whiny rock stars than taking care of his only son—to pick them up from the ArcLight after they'd gone to see the new *Harry Potter* movie together. They hadn't told their friends, who said the movie was dorky. That was okay though; it was their secret. Myla was in the middle of a rant about how she sometimes hated the ArcLight's assigned seats— the Hogwarts-uniformed senior citizen in the seat next to her and Ash had reeked of asparagus and Old Spice. That was when Ash leaned over and kissed her, right in front of the Cinerama Dome. They'd been Hollywood's youngest golden couple ever since.

And they were inseparable.

But Myla's parents—Barbar, as they were called by the press—had insisted on a family vacation this summer. "Vacation" meant a whirlwind tour of the third world, doing United Nations aid work at their older children's adopted countries: Thailand for Myla, Bangladesh for Mahalo, and Madagascar for Bobby, now six. Myla had to share a room with her two brothers—next to her parents and the three recently adopted toddlers—often in villages so small and remote she couldn't get a cell phone signal or Internet. She couldn't indulge in online retail therapy, take a real shower, update her Facebook status, or, more important, communicate with Ash. It was *torture*.

Granted, she could have called Ash every second while she was in Paris last week, visiting her old friend Isabelle, who'd moved there in fourth grade. But she'd been in the city of love without the love of her life—thinking about him too much would have depressed her. In a way, she also thought the waiting was romantic. Being some- one who never had to wait long for anything she wanted, Myla enjoyed the way her heart beat when she thought about her and Ash finally being together again.

She punched a string of numbers into her phone, twirling a lock of her long ebony hair around her index finger. She smiled, catching a glimpse of the shiny, emer- ald green streak that fell along the left side of her neck. It had been Ash's idea, and Myla had initially been revolted, but now she loved the secret burst of color.

Isabelle picked up on the third ring. "*Ma chère amie*, I missed you too."

Myla could hear the clinking of silverware and wine- glasses in the background. Even though it was after eleven there, Isabelle was probably just eating dinner now, before hitting Paris's nightclubs.

"Stop that, Guillaume!" Isabelle squealed delightedly to her boyfriend. "Sorry, he's being a total perv. Shouldn't you be with Ash?"

"He's late." Myla fiddled nervously with the plastic

Green Lantern bubble gum machine ring she wore on a Tiffany gold chain. She and Ash had traded rings from a bubble gum machine in ninth grade, and she had worn it on her neck ever since. Myla fully planned to hire Mindy Weiss, the best wedding planner in L.A., to work the cheap rings into the ceremony when they got married.

"Better he's late than you are, if you know what I mean," Isabelle said bawdily, before cracking up. "Oh, that's right! You haven't done it yet. *Quel dommage*."

Myla rolled her eyes. "We can't all be French sluts like you," she teased her friend.

A woman in a *Jesus Saves (Ask Me How)* T-shirt rumbled by, scowling at the dirty talk.

"I know, you're waiting for the right time." Isabelle yawned. "Just make sure to take advantage of being young and hot. Now go moisturize before he gets there."

Isabelle hung up with a giggle, probably to stop Guillaume's wandering hands again, and Myla hung up too. Two girls walked by arm in arm, wearing matching Fairy Princess T-shirts and glittery purple leggings.

Myla sighed. Even if they were only ten, you had to start learning the basic rules of fashion *sometime*. She yanked the pile of dog-eared *Vogues* from her bag and thrust the magazines into the taller girl's arms.

If thoughts of "stranger danger" occurred to either girl, they didn't show it. They studied Myla's round cheeks, smooth skin, and almond-shaped, shamrock-colored eyes. Recognition flashed across their surprised faces. They must have seen her photo in *People*, helping Barbar hand out care packages in the Philippines. And here she was again, doing charity work of her own.

Ash Gilmour was late for everything, a habit he'd never wanted to develop but had learned from his record impresario father. "Early means eager. Eager is weak," he'd always said.

But when it came to Myla Everhart, Ash *was* weak. And he'd wanted to be waiting at LAX when she'd landed. He wanted to watch her come down the escalator to the baggage claim, to see whatever impossible shoes she was wearing, followed by her long legs with the little birthmark below her right knee. Then her slim little body, and her tumble of hair with the green streak just for him. And then that face—lips that reminded him of the cherries on top of a sundae and eyes that always looked a little sleepy but saw every little thing.

Ash parked his vintage black 1969 Camaro and stumbled out, half-running across the wide one-way street reserved for shuttle buses and taxis. He dashed past planters of daisies lining the median and skidded to a stop in his beat-up Vans. On the drive over, he'd called House of Petals to get Myla's favorite hot pink peony bouquet, but they'd been crazed with some Endeavor agent's wedding. He reached down and picked six daisies, then sprinted across the rest of the street, nearly getting hit by a limo driver.

Safely on the sidewalk, Ash composed himself, shoving his shaggy dark blond hair off his forehead and smoothing his vintage Zeppelin tee. He stepped through the automatic doors. The air-conditioning swallowed him, but he saw no sign of Myla on the benches or near the baggage carousel. He checked the arrivals board. Her flight had made it. Oh, shit. How late was he? Had she left without him?

Myla was in the LAX ladies room, applying a final coat of Urban Decay XXX gloss in Baked. Satisfied, she tossed her hair and headed for the door. Surely Ash would be here by *now.*

Swinging her bag back to her shoulder, she pushed through the doors to be greeted *not* by her boyfriend, but by four paparazzi.

"Myla, where's Barbar?"

Now that Myla was sixteen, and with her parents less, she got photographed more and more on her own. Some days she didn't mind it, but after a fourteen-hour flight? Come on.

She gave the photogs a sarcastic smile, knowing an unflattering scowl would certainly make the tabloids. "Take your pick: Adopting a baby from a war-torn region. Building houses in a hurricane-ravaged stretch of the South. Having wild, passionate affairs with their costars."

A photographer sporting a jet-black goatee asked, "Are they here, Myla? You can tell us." His eyes were focused on Myla's toned thighs.

Myla raised her eyebrows. "First, take a picture, it lasts longer. Which you should already know. Second, no, my parents are not here. Now please get out of my way." They fired a few more shots and were gone. Myla blinked post-flashbulb into the crowd of new arrivals.

And then she saw him.

There, clutching a sad bouquet of crumpled daisies, was Ash. His sun-lightened hair hung shaggily over his ears, and his chestnut-colored eyes looked like a heart-broken puppy's. She stopped where she stood, waiting for him to come to her.

Ash, meanwhile, felt like he'd been kicked in the stomach. Where was Myla? He began to look carefully around the crowded terminal. A British tour group ambled slowly to the baggage claim on his right. To his left, he saw nothing but a cluster of Japanese business-men. Straight ahead, he studied girls at the newsstand, flipping through copies of *W*. A girl with long, shiny black hair had her face buried in *Vogue*. She looked up, and Ash saw she was probably thirty. Where was Myla? He felt like he might cry, something he hadn't done since his grade-school friend Jacob Porter-Goldsmith spilled Sunny D on Ash's favorite Pokémon card.

Then Ash noticed a small group of scuzzy-looking paparazzi walking away from the ladies' room corridor. As they parted, he finally saw her. There was Myla, wear-ing the world's shortest dress, her slim legs tanned and sexy above a pair of crazy-high shoes. She tilted her head at a "come and get me" angle. Her dark hair tumbled over the straps of her big plum-colored bag. She grinned and took a few steps closer.

He nearly tripped over his navy blue Vans trying to reach her faster. When he did, he lifted her into the air, dropping the daisies to the polished airport floor. And with hundreds of travelers and tourists surrounding them, he kissed her like it was the only thing he ever needed to be good at in his whole life.

Myla was only vaguely conscious that the paparazzi were shooting photos of them. Their reunion wouldn't make a cover, but because of her parents, they'd get an inset box. She could see the caption now: *Hollywood's Princess finds her Prince Charming*.

A WHOLE NEW WORLD

Josephine Milford—Jojo to anyone who wanted to stay on her good side—tossed another Roxy hoodie atop the mountainous pile of clothing in the center of her sustainable-bamboo bed. She heaved a sigh, then gathered her thick brown hair into a ponytail at the top of her head. Her room was stuffy, since her parents refused to set the AC below eighty-four degrees. She was already sweating in her JFK High soccer shorts and tank top.

Jojo was packing for Greenland, of all places, and she wasn't having an easy go of it. Her wardrobe go-to's—American Eagle miniskirts, Aéropostale tank tops, lightweight cotton T-shirts, and her most flattering Gap V-neck—didn't exactly scream "ice-bound continent!" Sure, her parents were on their sabbatical from UC Sacramento, but who took a sixteen-year-old girl to Greenland for her pivotal junior year?

She turned to her mirrored closet door, wondering how she would look after a semester in the snow. Her olive skin, a deep brown thanks to a summer of soccer practice, would probably fade to pale and pasty. Her pink lips would become chapped and wintry. Hopefully, her violet blue eyes wouldn't freeze shut as she cried away her school year in Greenland's frigid tundra. They would be living in Nuuk, the country's capital, but it wasn't exactly cosmopolitan.

Jojo stuck out her tongue at her reflection as she waited for best friend, Willa Barnes, to come back to the phone. They were discussing the tragic way Jojo would be spending the next nine months.

"Sorry about that," Willa finally breathed into the phone. "Damian put his turtle in the toilet bowl."

Jojo would babysit Willa's five-year-old brother Damian until she turned fifty if it meant she could stay in Sacramento. Not that it was the capital of cool or anything, but it was better than Nuuk. At least she had friends here. Plus, she'd just made forward on the soccer team.

"You know that cute miniskirt I bought at Bebe?" Jojo looked longingly at her short, red A-line skirt with oversize front pockets. She pulled it on over her soccer shorts and admired her tanned calves in the mirror. "Do you want to adopt it?" She sighed, yanking the skirt off and throwing it into a separate pile on her bed. "I don't think Greenland is miniskirt territory."

Willa laughed. "There might be cute Greenlandian guys desperate to see a girl wearing something totally inappropriate in the snow."

Jojo flopped onto her bed, picking up the latest *Us Weekly*. Barbar and their kids were on the cover with three Bangladesh villagers. Their oldest daughter—a gorgeous Thai sixteen-year-old—wore a green Versace halter and a pair of True Religion cutoffs. Jojo figured the cost of the girl's skimpy outfit alone could probably feed all the starving kids on those late-night "this child needs your help" commercials. She tossed the magazine on her desk with the stack of books she'd probably read within the first week of boring Greenlandian life.

"Maybe it will have globally warmed by the time you get there," Willa reasoned.

"I've never wanted the Earth to die more." Jojo sighed. She looked out her window, imagining Justin Klatch, the captain of the boys' soccer team, pulling his blue Scion up in front of the house to appeal to her parents for mercy. She'd only had the guts to make eye contact with him once in her whole life. But maybe by some miracle he was in love with Jojo too, and needed her to stay in Sacramento. If they took her away now, he'd become a recluse, not even leaving his house for soccer games. Maybe hearing his desperate pleas, her parents would relent. . . .

There was a knock at Jojo's door.

"Gotta go." Jojo quickly dropped the phone on her nightstand and picked up a pair of jeans. She was supposed to be packing, not chatting. Pretending to fold them, she yelled, "Come in!" to her dads.

Yes, dads. Plural.

Frederick and Bradley Milford shuffled into her room, looking like cover models for the Nonthreatening Gay Men Catalog. Even in balmy August, they wore itchy wool sweater vests. Fred's was a little snug around his potato-sack upper body. Bradley, rail-thin and a head taller than Fred, carried a cup of his favorite free-trade coffee in a National Public Radio pledge drive mug.

"Hi," Jojo said innocently, gesturing to the pile of to-pack items. "Look at all my progress."

Fred looked at her over the top of his horn-rimmed glasses. "Jojo, can we have a chat?"

She shoved the pile of clothing from her bed, revealing the organic cotton bedspread. "Go for it."

Fred and Bradley sat and Jojo pulled out her IKEA desk chair. She plopped onto it backwards, resting her chin on the seat back. "What's up? Greenland called and canceled? We're ruining my social life and potential for teenage normalcy in Costa Rica instead?"

"No, this is serious," Fred said, tugging a loose thread on his sweater and admiring his new wedding ring. "Why don't you come sit over here?" He patted the bed between him and Bradley. Fred was short and bald, with chocolate skin and a soft, cuddly look to him. He always wanted to drop ten pounds, though he'd need to lose fifteen to make any difference.

Bradley, on the other hand, was pale and reedy, with pointy features and a wild tuft of blond hair that couldn't be controlled by even hair gel. Jojo knew this because she had tried.

She rolled her desk chair to the bed and, playing along, smushed herself between her dads. "Really, guys, is this going to be another 'you're a woman now' talk? 'Cause I'm totally cool on the tampon thing."

"We'll just say it, Josephine," Bradley began, running his long fingers along his corduroy shorts. She sat up a little straighter at the use of her full name. Had she gone over her cell phone minutes again?

Bradley took a deep breath, like he was about to run

a marathon. "Remember your tenth birthday?" he tentatively questioned.

"Yeah, my disastrous boy-girl party? With the two boys and thirteen girls?" Jojo rolled her eyes, remembering. "Oh, but the decorate-your-own-cupcake thing was cool."

"This is more about what we discussed on your birthday," Bradley continued, a serious edge in his voice. "How you'd be open to meeting your birth parents, if the opportunity arose."

Jojo gulped. She remembered the conversation vividly. She'd spent the week after that birthday wondering what her biological parents were like. She and Willa had even planned to take a road trip when they turned seventeen so that Jojo could meet them.

"We got a call from them yesterday." Fred placed his pudgy hand on Jojo's knee. "They've been looking for you for years."

Her birth parents? Looking for her for years?

"They found us through the adoption agency. We spoke with them this morning," Fred went on.

The air around Jojo felt heavy. She stared at Bradley, then turned to face Fred.

Then she narrowed her eyes. "Wait a second. . . . Is this some weird surprise going-away-party thing? You'll tell me we're going to meet them and then we'll get over to Sadie's Pizza and all my friends will be there? Because that's a horrible prank."

Fred gave Bradley an uneasy look.

Jojo took it to mean this was *real*. She felt as though there were a strange hole somewhere between her chest and her stomach.

Her dads were studying her more closely than they did their pet avocado tree after a storm. "So what do they want from me?" she asked hesitantly, breaking the silence.

"Well, they'd like to meet you," Bradley said, playing with the corners of Jojo's *Us Weekly*. "And they were extremely nice on the phone, and seem to be, um, great with kids."

"The timing's messy," Fred chimed in. "But if you want to meet them, now's your chance. They've invited you for the weekend. You can go down there and we'll head to Greenland, get the new place set up before you get there. They've even offered to pay to change your ticket to Nuuk at the end of your stay. Only if you're comfortable with the idea of meeting them, of course."

Jojo reached for her beaten-up stuffed Fozzie Bear. She held it to her chest, squeezing. Parents. Her real parents. She stared at the silver-framed photo on her desk. It was from Fred and Bradley's wedding. In it, Jojo beamed as she stood between her dads, wearing her very own rental tux with baby blue cummerbund and bow tie. She'd been their best girl.

Her dads *were* her real parents. Right? So why couldn't she drown out the little voice in her head? She loved Fred and Bradley more than anything but—a mom? She'd always been a little envious of Willa. Willa's mom baked with her, made her Halloween costumes, took her shopping, and had totally helped Jojo with the whole tampon thing, truth be told.

Now she could have her own mom. True, she could be some awful bitch. Maybe she was a trash-tastic reality show contestant who just wanted to meet Jojo for added drama in the season finale. But maybe she was . . . normal?

"What are they like?" She grabbed Fred's pudgy arm, then withdrew it, worried her excitement would hurt her dads' feelings.

Bradley pushed his shock of blond hair down, wearing the same serious expression he'd worn when he came to Jojo's biology class to talk about deforestation. The dads shared another look.

When neither spoke, Jojo couldn't take it anymore. "Are they messed up? Are they in a cult or something? Are they deformed?"

Fred spoke carefully, his dark eyes showing no hint of this being a joke. "Actually, they're famous."

Jojo squeezed Fozzie. "Like they grew the world's biggest watermelon or something?"

"No, famous like . . ." Bradley pointed to the cover of Jojo's *Us Weekly*. Lailah Barton and Barkley Everhart held hands, fingers intertwined, as they gazed lovingly at a group of poverty-stricken Bangladeshi villagers. "Like Barbar famous."

She stared at the impossibly attractive people on the cover.

"No one is Barbar famous," Jojo said, incredulously. "Except Barbar."

"Well that's the thing." Fred grabbed her in a half hug. "That's them."

"Lailah and Barkley are your biological parents." Bradley hugged Jojo's other side, squishing her like a panini. "They're inviting you to stay at their house, in Beverly

Hills, for the weekend. It's a short flight." He pulled an envelope from his back pocket.

Jojo haltingly took it from Bradley's long fingers. She tore it open, her hands shaking. Inside was a plane ticket, leaving tomorrow for L.A.

First class.

She took one more look at her glamorous family on the cover of *Us*—Barkley, Lailah, and her, hmm, *sister* Myla. The world's most famous couple were . . . her mom and dad?

"I love you guys," Jojo said to her dads, and they enveloped her in a hug. "You'll always be my family, but I think I need to do this." From the tight, comforting grip of her fathers' arms, Jojo eyed her red miniskirt, sitting limply in the Willa adoption pile. The skirt was all wrong for Greenland.

But it would be perfect for Hollywood.

PARENTAL GUIDANCE IS SUGGESTED

"Jonathan, you turn right at Sepulveda!"

"Gigi, I know where I'm going. Right, and we'll be smack back where we came from."

"I told you we should have taken the 405."

"Geeg, you complain about the 405 every night. Why would I subject myself to that?"

Jacob Porter-Goldsmith sat in the backseat of his parents' XTerra, trying to determine whether his athletic-cut tee was tighter around the arms. He'd done an extra set of curls every night this week. It had to be tighter. Definitely.

His mom, Gigi, turned around in the passenger seat. "Jacob, smile for me."

"What are you talking about?" He studied his mom's freckled face, framed with a halo of frizzy auburn hair.

"Smile for me this instant," she said in the same sharp tone she used with members of the press when they published off-the-record information. A publicist who specialized in Hollywood's rising young stars and falling older ones, Gigi Porter was fierce about protecting her clients' privacy—at least when they wanted her to.

Jacob stretched his mouth wide open.

"Still straight," Gigi pronounced, seeming to count each of Jacob's teeth to make sure they were all there. "That bastard orthodontist. I should report him to the ADA."

Jacob's braces had come off just before he left for Brighton, Massachusetts, to work as a camp counselor for Benjamin Gompertz Machenah, a Jewish math camp. He'd worn the big old-fashioned metal braces for five years, while his mom had paid the orthodontist $150 a month to seemingly look at Jacob's mouth and say, "Keep it up." On what had been supposed to be his braces removal day, his orthodontist had said he needed one more year. His mom had cried foul and demanded they come off that day—it *had* been half a decade. The orthodontist, a cocky former stuntman with hands more suited to pounding faces than straightening teeth, had done it, warning, "I won't guarantee the work. His mouth will be a mess again in a month." So far, Jacob's teeth were fine. Actually, better than fine, with faithful use of the Crest Whitestrips he'd picked up at the Brighton Walgreens.

"Can you believe that? His teeth are gorgeous. Gorgeous! Jonathan, are you listening to me?" Gigi glared at his father, who was the world's calmest Los Angeles driver. As a rabbi "with occasional Buddhist tendencies," Jonathan Goldsmith prided himself on being accepting of all life's misgivings.

"They are gorgeous, Geeg," Jonathan said evenly, massaging his salt-and-pepper beard. "The boy's filled out over the summer, too."

Jacob wished he hadn't used his whole iPod battery on the plane to Burbank. He could have listened to the Hold Steady instead of his parents talking about him like he wasn't there. He stared out the window, watching as a Lexus sedan full of Beverly Hills High senior girls pulled up to the red light on Wilshire. The driver was a girl named Mina, a Jessica Simpson look-alike whom his best friend, Miles Abelson, had once asked to be his date to a *Battlestar Galactica* convention. She'd said no, of course.

Kids at BHH called Miles "McNothin'," because he looked just like that kid McLovin' from *Superbad* but had even less game. Jacob couldn't really knock him for it though: His own BHH nickname was "PG," for two reasons: they were his last two initials, and some BHH jocks had witnessed him getting turned away from *Spider-Man 3*, which was rated PG-13. Jacob had been fourteen at the time. Yes, he was that weak. This year would be different, though. It had to be.

"His hair's awfully long." Jacob's mom was eyeing him in the rearview mirror again.

He smoothed his hair down. "No haircuts," he said, turning back to look out the window at the carful of girls.

Mina turned her head, presumably to check her flaw-lessly curled blond hair and makeup in the rearview mir-ror. She caught Jacob staring and smirked. But there was something different about the look. . . .

It wasn't the usual, "whatever, geek" smirk. She didn't recognize him. And if Jacob wasn't mistaken, her smirk was saying, *You might be all right if you weren't riding in your parents' backseat.*

As the light changed and she pulled away, Jacob felt pretty good. The twenty pounds of muscle he'd added over the summer had filled out his formerly long, bony face. He'd finally made peace with his Jewfro—the curly mop he'd inherited from his dad that his mom now said was too long. Thanks to guys like Seth Rogen—whom his mom happened to represent—Jacob's hair was au courant instead of hopeless. He'd tried to hide all vestiges of nerd-dom: he'd only brought two volumes of *Sandman* with him to camp, trying to listen to cool music he'd read about in *Spin* instead. And he'd *barely* looked at the camera phone photos Miles had sent him last month from Comic-Con. Well, he'd looked but deleted all but one, a cute close-up of Katee Sackhoff. Lastly, he was *Jake* now, not Jacob. Jacob was a guy who jocks messed with and girls ignored. Jake was a guy who messed with girls and jocks admired.

"I wish your brother had come home today too." Gigi sighed. "I really don't want to make that trip again." Jake's younger brother, Brendan, had been at Camp Koufax, a Jewish baseball camp in upstate New York, and would miss his first week of eighth grade to play in a championship tournament against Camp Greenberg.

His dad turned down Bedford. Almost home.

Gigi sighed in relief, happy to be nearing the house. She didn't like long car rides, plane trips, or anything that required her to stay in one spot for more than an hour. "I have to tell him, Jonathan. I can't wait," Gigi said, practically hopping up and down on her seat like a little kid. Since she'd quit smoking, Gigi fidgeted more than ever.

Jacob groaned and sank lower in the standard-issue gray fabric seat. He hated his parents' surprises: Last summer, he'd gone to science camp at Berkeley and had come home to a Segway scooter. Not wanting to be ridiculed, Jacob had rewired it so it only ran in reverse. Gigi had bombarded the company with angry letters.

"Geeg, we're almost home, just wait."

"Jacob, we got you a car!" Gigi whipped around in her seat, her dark eyes bugging out of her head. Jonathan shook his head in disappointment, his eyes never leaving the road.

Jacob sprang from his slouch, practically jumping into the front seat. "You're kidding."

Images of a sleek black Range Rover filled Jacob's head. Or a cool vintage car, like a Camaro, even if his next-door neighbor and former childhood best friend Ash Gilmour already had one. No, no, an Escalade would be much better. Jacob pictured himself pulling up next to Ash's car in one three times its size with a girlfriend one hundred times hotter than Myla Everhart in his passenger seat.

"After all, you need a way to get to tutoring," his mom pointed out, the words instantly killing Jacob's high.

Before he'd left for camp, he'd been recruited by Sum of Us, a countywide tutoring network, to assist L.A. students who needed one-on-one help in math. Jake had been flattered in the spring. But after a summer spent with math nerds of the first degree, forget it. Working as a counselor at math camp all the way across the country he could handle. There, he was the cool guy. But tutoring in such a public way at BHH was like announcing to the world, *Yes, I suck at sports, my mom buys all my clothes, and I've only kissed a girl if you count the druid I met on a World of Warcraft quest.*

"Mom, Dad, about tutoring," he began, running a hand through his hair. "I just don't think I'll have time this year. I'll have the SATs. Some of the counselors said verbal was really rough."

"BS," was all his mother could say. His father shook his head and pulled the car over to the curb, a block from their house. Jacob exhaled loudly and tugged his hair down against his scalp. He wanted to get home already and see his car.

"You want out now because you think it's nerdy," his father said in his Wise Rabbi voice, his hazel eyes examining Jake in the rearview mirror. "But what's truly nerdy is not honoring your commitments."

"And not having a car," Gigi bargained, the way she played hardball with studio heads. "No tutoring, no car."

Jacob gave up, flopping back onto his seat. He hated that his parents could see through him so easily.

"Fine, I'll tutor," he said, knowing he wouldn't win this fight if his parents were allied against him. "If I can ever see this mythical car you're holding over my head."

His dad pulled away from the curb and finished the trek back to their two-story Spanish Revival–style home. Its facade gleamed white, the bay windows twinkling in the sun. The house wasn't much bigger than the average Santa Clarita McMansion, but with its Beverly Hills address it was worth about six of those homes.

Before his dad had even parked fully, Jake jumped out of the car and sprinted to the driveway. Parked outside the two-car garage was a car.

Not an Escalade. Not a Land Rover. Not a Mini. Not even a copy of his dad's XTerra.

It was the dirtiest powder blue Toyota Corolla Jake had ever seen.

"It's Grandma's," his dad said, coming up behind him. "Hardly any miles on it. But it could use a wash."

Jacob shook his head, wondering how he'd convinced himself his parents would buy him a luxury vehicle when their favorite pastime was teaching him the value of money. He shrugged, eyeballing the Corolla for dents. It looked healthy enough. Old, yes. Ugly, yes. His grandmother's at some point? Yes. But it was all his.

Within minutes, Jake had the hose, a bucket of soapy water, and a can of Turtle Wax laid out in front of the car. He sprayed the car with water, watching with satisfaction as the dirt melted away. Sponging soapy water over the car's hood, he began to sweat in the unforgiving August sun almost instantly.

The old Jacob would have abandoned his work to log some World of Warcraft hours in the air-conditioned house. New and improved Jake had no problem taking off his shirt and putting some muscle behind his work.

His rinse done, he applied Turtle Wax to every square inch of the Corolla, using the same precision he'd previously given to painting miniature medieval soldiers, his sixth-grade hobby. He whistled while he worked. Over his version of *The Simpsons* theme song, he heard a car slow on Bedford. He looked up to see Mina and her gang of BHH hotties.

"Nice," she said, her throaty voice floating through the stagnant summer air. "Woo-woo!" Her trio of friends gave a cheer as Mina honked and sped away.

Jacob raised an eyebrow at himself in the car's now-shiny hood. Muscles? Check. Car? Check. Girlfriend? It wouldn't be long now. . . .

HOLLYWOOD FOOD CHAIN

"You are Barbar's daughter," Jojo said to herself, staring at her violet blue eyes in the mirror of the first-class passenger lavatory. In less than an hour she'd be face-to-face with Lailah Barton and Barkley Everhart, the most bankable and most charitable actors in all of Hollywood.

They were also her birth parents. They'd sought her out. So what happened if they didn't like her? Would they send her back?

Jojo practiced her best pouty-lipped, come-hither look in the mirror. Nope, she didn't resemble her mom, Lailah. She tried a half-smirk with a hint of playful mischief. No sign of Barkley's genes either. She just looked constipated. Next, she tried her best "buy a candy bar, it's for my soccer team" smile. That was a little better. They'd go for that, right?

"Hi, Mr. Everhart, Ms. Barton, my name is Jojo," she tried, sticking out her hand for a fake handshake. No, too first-day-of-school. "Mom, Dad. I'm your daughter, Josephine." She shook her head. Too Lifetime movie.

Jojo turned on the tap and washed her hands. At least

she was happy with her outfit: her favorite black Gap V-neck, newest Abercrombie dark wash jeans, and silver Steve Madden ballet flats. She'd decided her new red mini made her look too much like an actress wannabe, fresh from a flyover state. Out of habit, she'd put her straight, chocolate brown hair up in a ponytail.

There was a knock at the door. "One second," Jojo called, annoyed that even in first class, there was a line for the bathroom.

"We're preparing to land, sweetie," singsonged the male flight attendant. Had she been in here that long? Jojo zipped her purse and left the bathroom. As she walked back to her seat, she noticed a blonde in the third row reading the *Us Weekly* with Barbar on the cover. The girl looked like Kirsten Dunst. As Jojo passed, she realized it *was* Kirsten Dunst, reading about *her* parents. It was surreal. Last week, her biggest goal had been to talk to Justin Klatch without saying anything stupid. This week, she'd landed at the top of the Hollywood food chain.

Fifteen minutes later, Jojo emerged from the plane. The Burbank Airport still had wheelie stairs that rolled up to the plane door. She gazed at the mountains in front of her and tasted the hot, dry air. A short man wearing a chauffeur outfit—complete with white gloves and a black, short-brimmed hat with gold piping—held a sign reading JOSEPHINE MILFORD. People really still did that? Jojo grinned. He tipped his cap to her.

She followed him as he crossed the tarmac and wove through the small airport, which was full of weekend travelers, many of them bleary-eyed and wearing souvenir

Las Vegas T-shirts. As they emerged outside, she spotted a shiny black hybrid SUV with tinted windows in the airport turnaround.

Jojo squeezed her eyelids shut, expecting that when she opened them, she'd wake up under her scratchy comforter in Sacramento, a trail of drool on Fozzie Bear's black plastic nose. Slowly, she lifted her lids: The SUV was still there. She stared at the tinted windows, unable to see anything through the glass.

This was it. Her parents—her *birth* parents—were in there, waiting to see her for the first time.

She breathed in the dry air. Tugging her black cotton tee to straighten the seam, Jojo edged toward the waiting SUV. "Stay calm," she muttered to herself, praying she wouldn't trip.

The driver reached the car first, swiftly tossing Jojo's bag into the trunk. He moved to the back passenger door and nodded at her, his hand on the door handle. Jojo took a deep breath and hurled herself into the backseat, a set of two long benches that faced each other.

As the car pulled away from the curb, she looked up to see two very familiar faces.

Ho. Ly. Shit.

Lailah Barton and Barkley Everhart sat less than an inch apart on the leather seat across from her, hands clasped as they stared at Jojo. Lailah's dark tumble of hair fell loosely against the neckline of a white boatneck sweater, her famous eyes hidden behind a pair of gold Hermès aviator sunglasses. Her long, toned legs were crossed neatly at the ankle, though she nervously jiggled a Manolo-clad foot. Next to her, Barkley, in a pair of jeans and a white button-down, was all shoulders and chis-eled jaw, his boyishly rumpled dirty blond hair looking like it needed a trim.

In sixteen years of living in Sacramento, Jojo had racked up three celebrity sightings: (1) Gwen Stefani, but it didn't count since she and Willa had paid to see her in concert; (2) some skinny dude from an ancient season of the *Real World*, who'd come to their school to talk about drugs; and (3) the back of Governor Arnold Schwarzenegger, during a field trip to the state capitol building.

Now she was sitting across from the king and queen of Hollywood. Also known as Mom and Dad.

"Barbar," Jojo said to herself, except she accidentally said it aloud. She winced. All those pep talks in the mirror, and she'd seriously just said her parents' tabloid nickname to their faces? She wondered how fast the car was moving, and if it was safe to jump out.

Lailah pulled off her sunglasses, probably to stare Jojo down as she politely asked her to leave.

But then Barkley smiled, displaying his famous dimple. Lailah's stunning violet blue eyes—just like *hers*, Jojo realized—misted over.

"Mom and Dad is fine . . . Josephine." Barkley chuckled as Lailah tightened her grip on his hand.

"If you're comfortable with that, of course," Lailah added, her eyes hopeful beneath a dark fringe of lashes.

And then it hit her: They were nervous, too. Lailah's foot was still jiggling, and Barkley looked like he had a metal rod for a spine. Jojo was surprised she couldn't hear their hearts beating across the backseat.

She grinned, suddenly at ease. "Mom and Dad is great. And you can call me Jojo."

At that, her parents' tentative expressions faded. Before Jojo knew what was happening, Barkley and Lailah were on her side of the aisle, folding themselves into seats on either side of her.

"We're so glad you're here," Lailah breathed, her graceful hand touching Jojo's hair.

"I still can't believe it," Barkley said, tenderly grabbing Jojo's hand.

And then, without asking permission—because it hardly seemed necessary—her parents wrapped her up in a tight, breathless hug.

Even though Sacramento was hundreds of miles away, this felt oddly familiar. It felt like coming home.

CAN'T GET NO SATISFACTION

Ash rolled over on his maroon sheets, thin rays of sunlight poking through his blinds. He didn't want it to be Sunday. From Friday afternoon on, his life had been perfect. Why spoil it?

He inched closer to Myla's lithe frame, careful not to wake her. She'd been napping on and off since she got back, and he loved watching her sleep. Even better was when she woke up in a haze and they kissed and cuddled and ate takeout from the Ivy off Lucite trays in Ash's bed. He loved having her all to himself, too: Myla had set her phone to go straight to voice mail so her gossipy friends couldn't reach her.

Her back was to him, her shiny, long hair splayed across the pillow. Ash gently ran his fingertips over it. It had never felt as soft as it did today. Though he knew it was probably just her Bumble and Bumble Creme de Coco masque, Ash felt like her hair had softened from being within his reach again.

Myla was the person he talked to, hung out with, his best friend. Not having her around all summer had meant he was bored, especially since everyone else had been traveling or working as interns in the "development" departments of their parents' studios, agencies, and production companies. Ash had tried to swing an internship at his dad's label, More Records, but his father hadn't wanted him on board. *"An internship? You mean free labor? I'd be getting what I paid for, wouldn't I?"* Gordon Gilmour prided himself on such choice nuggets of wisdom, dispensed in short bursts during the infrequent cell phone conversations he had with his son. For his part, Ash hadn't tried all that hard to convince his dad to give him a job. He was seventeen. He had music to listen to, rock bands to dream up, and the occasional waves to surf. Who needed a job?

Still, Ash had gotten lonely. Really lonely. Gordon lived in Malibu with his new supermodel wife and their two young kids, leaving Ash practically alone in the Italian Renaissance–style home Gordon still kept in Beverly Hills. After divorcing his dad, Ash's mom had moved to Austin, Texas, capitalizing on her ex-husband's music scene credibility to start the Gilmour, a music venue for hot underground rock bands. His older sister, Tessa, had chosen to stay in Berkeley for the summer—she'd be a junior there this fall. For three whole months, Ash had felt like an island, actually looking forward to the days the maids came to clean. A guy could only get baked and play "Stairway to Heaven" on Rock Band so many times.

Ash lay back down on his pillow, wishing he and Myla had more time before school started tomorrow. They hadn't gotten to do any of their usual summer stuff, like throwing huge theme parties at Ash's house, going to concerts at the Roxy and the Troubadour, floating on rafts in Myla's pool, and drinking cocktails they'd invented themselves. Plus, he'd finally gotten his license. They could have road-tripped to Coachella this summer instead of having one of their drivers take them.

Myla stirred, rolling onto her back, her chest barely covered by her Hanky Panky lace cami. Even though Myla was self-conscious about her small chest, Ash loved it. She reminded him of one of those 1960s mod girls, with the little dresses and the go-go boots. Ash had a thing for girls in boots. Maybe from all the superhero comics he'd read back when he still hung out with his next-door neighbor Jacob.

"Morning," Myla said, half-opening her green eyes.

"Morning, you." Ash reached for the strand of green hair right at the nape of her neck. He'd been relieved at the airport to see it was still there, and that she still wore her Green Lantern ring on the chain around her neck. After a summer of barely hearing from her, part of him had worried she'd moved on. "Still jet-lagged?"

Myla shook her head. "I finally feel like a human again."

"You still haven't told me about your trip, what you saw, what you did." Ash laughed suggestively—they had been too busy getting reacquainted in other ways. Well, not *that* way—he and Myla hadn't done it yet. But soon. He was sure of it. They would be ready.

"Do good this, do good that." Myla yawned. "Blah, blah, blah. Then seven actually fun days in Paris. Isabelle says hi, by the way."

"Oh." Ash lazily rubbed the soft skin in the bend of Myla's elbow. His eyes fell on the webcam he'd bought her for her Mac Air laptop. He'd asked for an address where he could mail it this summer—he'd wanted to talk to her, face-to-pixelated-face, on their anniversary—but she'd never responded. He'd also bought a promise ring, a platinum and emerald version of Myla's bubble gum ring, that he'd planned to give to her over the webcam.

"Oh yeah, happy anniversary," he said, hating how whiny his voice sounded. "July twenty-first. Three years." He felt like a baby, but saying the words out loud made him feel as alone and frustrated as he had on the actual day of their anniversary. He'd sat waiting at his computer for some acknowledgment of his e-mail, but Myla had been MIA. Like she'd been all summer long.

Myla sat up, the covers rumpled around her waist, instantly defensive. She'd actually sat around at a crappy Internet café all day on the twenty-first, feeling neglected and sad. What she hadn't realized—until her mom laughingly pointed it out—was that because of the time difference it was still the twentieth for Ash. She would have written him, but he was supposed to come to her. She was the one suffering thousands of miles away, not him. Then, on the right day, she'd been traveling by Jeep to Bobby's mud-hut village, and she hadn't been able to get back online for a week. Plus, her family kept going from one place to the next, so she never had even a semipermanent address for the camera Ash wanted to send. "I didn't forget. That was the same day Bobby met his parents in some crazy village in Madagascar. Outside Betatao or something like that. Even dial-up was impossible, or I would have e-mailed you back sooner. I'm sorry."

Ash, still in just his hunter green boxer briefs, rose

from the bed and walked over to his desk, wishing he hadn't mentioned their anniversary at all. He flopped down in his Aeron chair in front of his MacBook Pro, slouching dramatically with his back to her. "Whatever. Let's not fight."

Myla reached for her bag, grabbing her James Perse tee and throwing it on over her underwear. She wanted to pull Ash's stupid floppy hair right now, he was being such a baby. She was the one who'd spent her summer sleeping under mosquito nets and craving iced blendeds. Like she'd wanted to spend her summer vacation a million miles away from her boyfriend. "What do you want from me?" She stood up, pulling her shirt down so it covered her boy shorts. "I tried."

Ash just stared at his Facebook page. "Yeah, you tried," he finally said, not looking at her as he clicked through his friend Tucker's photos from Rome.

Myla flopped down on the bed, twirling her ring around on its gold chain. She was back for thirty-six hours, and he was trying to drag her into an argument? No way. Today all she wanted was to watch movies in Ash's dad's super-air-conditioned screening room, cuddling and feeding Ash popcorn.

"You know, up until now I thought *I* was the girl in this relationship," Myla teased, walking up behind Ash and putting her hands on his bare shoulders. "But you're acting kinda needy."

Ash shook her off, his eyes still centered on his screen. He started checking his Gmail.

Myla felt irritation prickle her caffeine-deprived skin and pulled her hands away. What was his problem? A good boyfriend would have planned some amazing welcome-home day for her, but Ash wanted to sulk? "Just because you had nothing to do all summer, don't take it out on me."

"I was busy," Ash countered, picking up a shirt off the floor and pulling it on. "Busy thinking about you, since you didn't keep in touch."

Myla turned to face him. With her hand on her hip, she was framed perfectly in Ash's closet mirror, so he could get an eyeful of her front and back. It would have made a cool album cover, Ash thought, if she wasn't so obviously pissed off.

"I'm so sorry your social life sucks so bad that because I couldn't get a fucking Internet connection in New Delhi you were like . . . bored." *Take that, you codependent baby,* she thought. Her eyes landed on Ash's guitar stand. Hanging from it was a beat-up Rolling Stones shirt that was a memento from their first date, a concert they'd gone to in eighth grade. They'd gone to the Avalon to see the Rolling Stones play a secret set for a very small crowd. It was Myla's first concert. She and Ash had gone backstage and met the whole band, who were totally old and a little gross but had been really nice and signed the shirt for them. An aspiring rocker, Ash had been in heaven, but he'd said they should share the shirt from then on. It wasn't the most flattering thing, but she loved to wear it. The scent of Ash's room clung to its soft cotton, making it beyond comforting.

Ash brushed her off. He sat back down at the computer, turning away from her again. "Don't worry about my social life. I had plenty of opportunities."

"What opportunities? Tucker and Geoff were in Rome, so I know they didn't invite you to some radical bong-smoking fest with those Circle K burnouts in Culver City." She shook out her jeans with a snap to punctuate the statement. Tucker Swanson and Geoff Schaffer were Ash's closest friends, and the ones Myla disliked most.

"No, not Geoff and Tucker. Cassie Eastman." Ash half-spun in his chair, sounding pleased with himself.

Myla thought of the big-chested blonde in their class at BHH. "Easy Eastman?" she asked, hoping that she sounded derisive rather than scared. Ash couldn't have been hanging out with that skank, could he? She started to pull on her jeans, quickly realizing they were backwards.

"Call her whatever bitchy nickname you want," Ash said coolly. If he just kept his voice mellow, Myla would get really worked up and jealous. Then he would confess that nothing had happened with Cassie. He had bumped into her at the Barnes & Noble at the Grove, and she'd practically undressed while hitting on him. If that weren't gross enough, he'd been instantly turned off when he saw her carrying Clay Aiken's new CD. Besides, she was no Myla.

Myla righted her pants. Had Ash really hooked up with Cassie Eastman? Myla knew that Ash had been waiting a long time to have sex. But would he just throw away their history for a good time with the least challenging girl at BHH? "At least my boobs are real," she spat. It was the best she could think of.

"Really nonexistent, maybe," Ash said, immediately regretting it.

Myla felt like she'd been slapped. He *knew* that would hurt. He could joke around about her family, her personality, even—on rare occasions—her taste in shoes. But rule number one was you did *not* dwell on her membership in the Itty-Bitty Titty Committee. Myla bit her lip, fighting back tears. At least he was showing what he really thought about her body. She'd spent all summer wishing she wasn't thousands of miles from Ash, and he'd spent the summer hitting on other girls? "Why don't you call Cassie, then? She sounds like the skank of your dreams," she muttered, trying to keep her voice from cracking.

"You know what? Maybe I will." Ash inched to the corner of his room where his guitar stand stood. On it hung their shared Rolling Stones shirt. He always put it on when he was having a bad day. It smelled flowery and sweet, like Myla.

"Are we done, Ash?" Myla took her phone from the nightstand and tossed it angrily into her bag, not looking at him.

Ash slumped onto his overstuffed hunter green couch, running his fingertips along the sage-tinted piping. He reached between the cushions, feeling the box that held the promise ring. He choked down the bile welling up in his throat, angrily squeezing the ring box. No way was he going to give Myla some huge, meaningful gift when she was ruining what was supposed to be an amazing reunion. And he was done with this stupid argument.

He nodded, slowly. "Yeah, just go."

Myla's knees trembled, and she fought to remain standing. Ash was supposed to rush to her. Embrace her.

Say, "I'm an idiot, Myla. I know you would have called if you could have. I'll make it up to you." Not *dump* her.

She coolly plucked the Rolling Stones shirt from the guitar stand, her face inscrutable.

Ash watched Myla, his stomach lurching. He thought he'd said yes to ending the argument, to Myla leaving until they both cooled off. But had he instead said yes to them breaking up?

"I guess that's that, then," she said, dropping the shirt into her vast bag. She vanished from Ash's room without turning back to look at him once.

"More couscous hash browns, Jojo? Or eggs Benedict?"

In all her screen roles, Lailah Barton had never served a soul. With a laser-beam stare that communicated sex, wealth, power, and steely determination, she was always believable as the woman who got what she wanted—top-secret information, the upper hand, the unattainable guy. And yet here she was, her dark hair pulled into a librarian's bun, holding a platter of eggs under Jojo's nose.

But Lailah Barton was no average suburban mom. With her hair up, Jojo could see Lailah's famed birthmark, a dark pink spot shaped like a near-perfect heart, at the base of her creamy neck. Her lips—naturally a dark, pomegranate red that L'Oreal had mimicked in its fall Lailah's Look line of cosmetics—formed a gentle smile.

"Or maybe you just want a steak?" Barkley Everhart grinned, his pool blue eyes alert. His famously muscular arms were lost beneath a too-big polo shirt and a Kiss the Cook apron, while a smear of steak sauce accentuated his dimpled cheek.

"Some hash browns and a steak sounds great," Jojo said, smiling. She wondered if Sunday brunch was always like this in the Everhart household, or if they'd gone all out for her.

She was sitting at the head—yes, the head—of a dining room table that she'd read about in *Us Weekly*. It was custom-made, and Barbar had had all of the family's names hand-carved into its baseboard. Right now, Jojo was running her finger along the *L* in *Lailah*. She'd seen photos of this room in *OK!* before: Three chandeliers, each ten feet across, hung from the fifteen-foot ceilings. Barbar had commissioned them from a sect of glass-blowing Tibetan monks. Along the wall across from Jojo was an heirloom china cabinet that Barkley had restored himself. The couple used it to display the kids' artwork. Front and center was a pretty decent crayon drawing of a brontosaurus with "Mahalo" scrawled in an eight-year-old's messy printing.

They'd spent the last twenty-four hours at home, since Lailah and Barkley had explained that fending off the paparazzi would cut into their time together. Jojo couldn't say she minded lying low at their Bel Air compound. When the driver had first pulled the hybrid SUV through the wrought-iron gates of the Everhart estate, Jojo had been awestruck, and nervous all over again. The house was, literally, a castle. Fashioned from custard-colored brick, it resembled a three-story dessert. Cylindrical towers, a circular window at the top of each, framed each side of the mansion. Spread out front was a magnificent French-style garden, replete with crimson tree roses and a duck pond. But now, Jojo felt more comfortable.

She could definitely get used to this. If she weren't leaving tomorrow, she reminded herself sadly.

She glanced around at her huge collection of siblings. Eight-year-old Mahalo's jet-black hair touched the collar of his vintage *Muppets* T-shirt, while six-year-old Bobby's tightly cropped curls hid beneath a knit cap. Ajani, Indigo, and Nelson—adopted from Cambodia, Ethopia, and India, respectively, all in the last two years—lined one side of the table in modern Swedish booster seats. Nelson, who had to be about three, proudly chomped on the cut-up chicken fingers his mom had set before him as Ajani and Indigo, each two years old, smushed couscous between their chubby fingers.

Mahalo gave Jojo a thumbs-up, grinning widely, while Barkley unloaded a giant filet mignon before her. Jojo smiled back. The kids had welcomed her warmly. Several times today, Mahalo had even led them in an improvised song—really just a chant of "Hello, Jojo"—that reached a fever pitch before they all erupted in giggles.

Lailah spooned some couscous onto the sliver of space left on Jojo's plate. "I'm sorry you haven't met Myla yet. She's with her boyfriend. They haven't seen each other all summer—"

"Hi guys, I'm home." Myla yawned sleepily as she made her way into the dining room. It was only one o'clock, but she fully planned to crawl under her Frette duvet as soon as possible. She smiled weakly at her siblings, trying to keep her eyelids at half-mast and look jet-lagged so she could go straight to her room.

After leaving Ash's this morning, she'd gotten a mani-pedi at Elle, then hit Barneys for some retail therapy. But the pampering and purchases hadn't elevated her mood. She'd been expecting Ash to call, apologizing for what happened and begging to make it up to her.

But he hadn't. Not yet, anyway. She told herself not to worry too much. Myla knew he'd come back, hot pink peonies in hand, eventually.

Suddenly her eyes fell on an unfamiliar face. There was a girl sitting in *her* chair. Her very special, oldest-sibling, head-of-the-table chair. The girl was pretty, with dark blue violet eyes, high cheekbones, and olive-colored skin. Myla narrowed her eyes, immediately shaken out of her jet-lagged act. Who was this person? The kids' nannies never ate with them.

"Myla, you're finally home," Lailah said, smiling. Her father, who'd been wiping egg yolk from Nelson's face, slung an arm around her mom's waist and pulled her to him. Lailah's free hand was on the girl's shoulder. Why was she touching the nanny?

"Myla, this is your sister Josephine," Barkley said. He chuckled nervously, shooting Jojo a sheepish smile. "Sorry. Jojo, she prefers Jojo."

Um, *sister*? Myla pulled tightly on her ring, the gold chain digging into the back of her neck. What. The. Fuck? Yes she had grown accustomed to sharing her parents with regular new family additions, but seriously? Her parents had only been home a week and they'd somehow managed to procure a new child?

Besides, this girl didn't look like some third-world refugee. Normally, there was the sympathy factor. But her V-neck shirt screamed "suburban mall," not "war-torn village."

"Hi." Jojo stood, crossing the expanse of dining room. She extended a hand. "It's great to meet you."

Myla shook Jojo's hand limply, putting on her fakest smile.

"Myla, why don't you sit down?" Lailah said, gesturing to a chair. "I'll get you something to eat."

Usually, her parents had a three-person kitchen staff to serve meals, but then, it wasn't every day they brought home a new kid. It just felt that way sometimes, Myla thought, looking around the table at Mahalo, Bobby, and the rest of the toddler U.N.

Myla sat in an empty chair next to the little girls. Indigo and Ajani, their ringlets in pigtails, wore matching poufy Fairy Princess party dresses—you couldn't get them to take those things off. Myla suppressed a grin, seeing her sisters and their tiny sparkle-polished fingernails. But no way would she let warm fuzzies interrupt her pissed-off mood.

She ignored the food on her plate, looking from Lailah to Barkley expectantly. They sat near Jojo, on the opposite side of the antiqued farmhouse table. Every so often they'd study Jojo, like she was some creature from another planet. *Well, it won't be long before they start adopting those, too,* Myla thought.

Barkley looked nervously around the table at his children. He cleared his throat and then cleared it again.

"It's awkward for me, talking about this, because I love your mother so much," Barkley said, his face focused on Myla's. "But you know I was married before. Well, when I met your mother."

Myla nodded. She really didn't need her dad's romantic

history right now. Anyone who'd so much as heard of *Us Weekly* knew about Barkley's first wife, Heather Merryton, America's sweetheart—whom Barkley had allegedly left for Lailah.

Her mom chimed in. "We couldn't help it. Your dad and I fell in love. And I got pregnant," she said, her eyes misty, like she was delivering an Oscar-worthy monologue. All she needed was a Dario Marianelli score behind her.

"Pregnant, pregnant," Nelson chimed in. "What pregnant?"

Lailah looked beatifically across the table at her three-year-old son, his dark curls in wisps around his face. "Shhh, honey, this is serious."

Myla almost burst out laughing. *Yeah, right.* Like the tabloids wouldn't have been all over her rising-star mom for having a baby on board. As it was, they were always hounding Barbar about whether they would have biological kids of their own. She could feel the words *prove it* on her tongue, but held back.

Lailah turned back to Myla, clutching Barkley's hand tightly. "I was twenty-two, and my career was just taking off," Lailah went on. "I couldn't be a homewrecker and pregnant to boot. We finished the movie, and I took a hiatus after I started to show. I went to live with some friends upstate, had the baby, and gave her up for adoption." Lailah looked at Jojo here, then quickly snapped her gaze back to Barkley. He squeezed her hand still tighter.

Nausea suddenly hit Myla, and it wasn't from the three iced blendeds she'd drunk at the Beverly Center.

This was starting to feel real, and she had an idea where it was headed. Myla gripped the edge of the table.

"Once my divorce was final, your mom and I got married. But we've always regretted giving that baby—you—up." Barkley was clutching Jojo's forearm tightly, as though he was afraid she'd get away.

Myla put her head against the back of her chair, feeling like she'd topple out of it if she didn't. Biological child. So it was true? Her parents, with their Multicultural Offspring Variety Pack, actually had a flesh-and-blood kid of their own?

And what did that mean for the rest of them?

Jojo, Barkley, and Lailah now formed a chain at one end of the table. "After dinner, I should dig up your birth certificate," Lailah finished, chuckling through the few tears that cascaded prettily down her cheek.

Barkley grinned. "It's the only one we've got that's in English."

Myla faked a laugh, wanting to pretend this was all okay with her. But her parents barely noticed. A kidnapper could have walked in, thrown a bag over her head, and carried her—kicking and screaming—out of the room and they wouldn't have glanced up from their new sixteen-year-old baby. Their *real* baby.

It wasn't fair. *Myla* was their first child—she had the *People* magazine spread on her adoption to prove it. They'd adopted her when she was four from a crappy orphanage in Mai Hong, Thailand. Barbar had been shooting their first international action thriller, *The Bangkok Project*, and had gone in search of jade jewelry for Lailah. A fisherman had given them lousy directions to the marketplace, and Barbar had gotten lost in the bustling village. They'd wound up on the doorstep of an orphanage, when their eyes had landed on Myla, small for her age, with a mass of dark hair and bright green eyes. It was adoption at first sight. On her birthdays, Barkley liked to hold his hands about a foot apart and joke with her, "I remember when you were only this big." Lailah once told Myla they'd almost named her Jade, because they'd never found the jewelry but had found a much better treasure. And she *was* their treasure. She was their first and—she always thought—their favorite. But now she knew the truth: She was just their rebound kid. The one they'd gotten impulsively, to help ease the pain of missing the one they *really* wanted. The one that was their own, not a third-world castoff.

Finally, when Barkley and Lailah were finished talking, Lailah sat down on one side of Jojo, looking across the table at her husband. "We hope you've had a good time this weekend, Jojo. And Myla would be happy to show you around next time," she added, smiling at her oldest daughter like they were all in this together.

"It's been amazing," Jojo gushed, meaning it. She couldn't finish her heaping plate of food, in part because she was so nervous about meeting Myla and in part because she was so sad at the prospect of leaving the next morning. "I only wish I didn't have to go to Nuuk tomorrow. I feel like I just got here. And Myla just got back." She smiled shyly at her new sister, but Myla was just staring at their parents, her face inscrutable.

At that, Barkley and Lailah exchanged a look.

"Well, we'd love to have you stay for a few more

weeks," Barkley said, beaming at her. "It's no problem for us, if your dads could spare you."

Lailah gazed at Barkley like she wanted to throw her arms around him in appreciation. She turned back to Jojo, her eyes hopeful. "If you like it here, you could even stay . . . longer?"

Her voice trailed off, but Jojo got the message. They were saying she could *live* here, in Beverly Hills, with the world's most beautiful couple—her parents—instead of in icy, barren Nuuk.

Myla's fingers curled around the cold steel of her fork. She got the message too.

100 PERCENT HEAVENLY

"*Reader, I married him.*"

Amelie had read the same line of *Jane Eyre* about a million times now, but she couldn't bring herself to concentrate on what was technically her favorite book. She'd never had this problem on the set of *Fairy Princess*, where she could polish off full chapters of classics between takes. But today was no day on the set of *Fairy Princess*. Today she was on the *Class Angel* set, which meant that Hunter Sparks was somewhere on the premises.

Kady Parker's loud, tinkling laugh rang out from across the soundstage. Amelie glanced at her, across the wide expanse of the Reavis High auditorium set. It took up most of the available space, and crepe streamers in navy and white hung from the basketball hoops. The wood-paneled floor shone under the overhead lights, a dark blue silhouette of a Reavis Knight painted in the center. On the auditorium's stage, a drum set and two guitars waited for the Creases, a new band that would play its hit single, "Drop It," in the movie.

Amelie sat with her back to the soundstage wall on one end of a set of bleachers. On the opposite end, Kady sat with DeAndra, Lina Colletti, Dani Mills, and the Lacey twins, who'd signed on for two days of shooting as backup bitchy cheerleaders. Kady wore her character's signature black hoodie.

Amelie was playing an angel sent to help Kady's mixed-up character buckle down and stay out of trouble, do well on the SATs, and get into art school. The script was eye-rollingly formulaic: Kady's punky loner got framed for stealing the school's treasured basketball trophy by a bitchy popular girl; then, with the assistance of a guardian angel and a sympathetic jock, she cleared her name and got the real villain in trouble. The producers had cast Amelie in the angel role to capitalize on her maturing *Fairy Princess* fans. Even though she'd secretly wanted Kady's part, Amelie contented herself that at least she was doing a movie set in a high school, rather than an enchanted forest.

Kady and the other girls had come late to the set after doing a sexy photo shoot for *EW* that morning, for a story titled "They're No Angels." It was about how Kady and Co. managed to live it up while still getting the job done, unlike past teen stars (who of course would not be named). Amelie thought it was a little premature for the magazine to go out on a limb like that, but maybe she was just jealous—she'd only done a five-question interview for an inset box, "100 Percent Heavenly." The reporter had asked things like, "Do you even know what's *in* a gin and tonic?"

Kady gave Amelie a little wave. It didn't feel like an invitation to come talk, though, so Amelie stayed put, glancing down at her weathered paperback. Kady and the other girls had been perfectly nice during lunch, sitting by Amelie as they nibbled on turkey-avocado wraps from Café Surfas and rehashed their latest nightclub adventures. Of course, their escapades sounded kind of fun, but Amelie wasn't about to take any chances. You didn't have a choice when your entire career was Fairy Princess. Little girls looked up to her. Her mom was proud of her. She knew better than to screw around, or she'd wind up on the Board.

The Board was a six-by-twelve-foot piece of corkboard in their upstairs den. On it, her mother had tirelessly pinned photos of child stars whose careers had gone awry. Along the top of the board were age markers: A star who at ten had been playing plucky twins in a Disney flick could be graphed to age sixteen as dating an older nightclub owner, to age eighteen as entering rehab for the first time, and to age twenty-two as being caught passed out and drooling on a chairlift in Aspen. Another Hollywood sweetheart, who'd gotten a start in sitcoms at age six, had gone platinum with innuendo-laden lyrics (and stripperlike dance moves) while professing her virginity at seventeen, married an ex-con (age eighteen), divorced (age nineteen), shoplifted at Target (age twenty), crashed her car into a 7-Eleven (twenty-one), and joined a cult (twenty-two). Amelie's timeline dated back to her debut, at two months old, as a Pampers model, and her trajectory was so far unmarred.

With the *Class Angel* part, the diapers were finally starting to come off. But that didn't mean Amelie wanted to jump from training pants to being photographed without underwear.

She buried her face in her book again, waiting while the crew hung more banners for the school dance scene. With every page she turned, her stomach twitched nervously. Where was Hunter? She'd checked the call sheet and discovered they had very few scenes together. Still, she'd hoped he'd stop by the set today. Amelie glanced at the digital clock near the camera setup. Five thirty. Day one was approaching the nine-hour mark, without so much as a trace of him.

"Amelie?"

She looked up to see the assistant director, Gary, standing in front of her, his ball cap pulled low over his messy brown hair. The AD was sort of the director's right hand, dealing with all the business needs of the film so the director could do the creative part. On *Class Angel*, Gary was doing almost everything. He had to: The actual director, Dirk Wink—who'd only scored the job because he'd gotten the right combination of execs beyond wasted at one of his debaucherous pool parties— could only be bothered to yell at the cast or mumble his coffee order to the production assistants.

"Yes?"

"We're going to move some things around," Gary said, his eyes droopy and red. He reminded Amelie of the basset hound she'd had as a kid. "We're skipping the cheerleader fight for now. We want to do the scene where Hunter sees Kady doing her community service at the dance. Think you can handle switching gears? In about fifteen minutes?"

She nodded, her stomach fluttering like the wings of Fairy Princess's favorite flying pony, Bubblelemon. "Sure, it's not a problem."

"I knew you'd say that." The AD jogged over to the director and camerapeople, giving a nod to go.

Hunter Sparks stood in the mock gymnasium, wearing a loose pair of vintage Levi's and a plain white tee. The cotton was thin enough that Amelie could almost see the abdominals *Shape* had devoted an entire feature to. She felt warm all over, and not just from the stifling heat. His dark hair was cropped close to his head, accentuating his strong, perfectly placed cheekbones. His eyes were the same rich brown as a dark chocolate cupcake from Sprinkles.

Unfortunately, Amelie wasn't supposed to be staring at Hunter in this scene—or any of her scenes. As Class Angel, she was invisible to him, and if they accidentally made eye contact, it would ruin the take. But Amelie didn't care how many takes it took. She kept sneaking glances at him, unable to believe he was really standing here, five feet from her.

"Okay, those last few lines once more," Gary hollered. They'd done seven takes of the school dance scene so far. It took place midway throughout the movie, when Lizzie Barnett, Kady's rebellious character, was still spurning the friendly advances of Tommy Archer, Hunter's jock.

Kady sighed, jumping around to loosen up behind the dance's refreshment table. Hunter, wearing a cheesy Homecoming King sash over his casual ensemble, cracked his neck and bounced on his toes. Amelie assumed the Class Angel position, standing behind Kady so she could rattle off heavenly lines of advice.

Extras milled around, most of them chatting with

their dance partners. The Creases held their instruments on stage, preparing to play—or rather, to pretend to play. Noise would have overpowered the actors' dialogue.

"Action," the AD called.

Extras started bobbing up and down to whatever tune they had playing in their heads. They'd do another take where the Creases actually played, so they could get their rhythm right. For now, it was only important that dancers were in the background.

"Look, I don't know why you have such a bug in your jockstrap," Lizzie snapped at Tommy, slapping a ladle of punch into a cup and handing it to a dancer. "I didn't steal the trophy, and I don't need your help. I'll get suspended or get out of it."

"He only wants to help," Class Angel cooed behind her. "Try not to be so crass." Amelie peered over Kady's shoulder, trying to exchange a look with Hunter, but he was so focused on the scene, they hadn't so much as made eye contact yet.

"Crass my ass. He's messing with me," Lizzie mumbled to Class Angel.

"What was that?" Tommy asked Lizzie curiously, his eyes dancing with interest. As per the script, Hunter stared in Amelie's direction but seemed to look right through her. Amelie felt a twinge of disappointment, but reminded herself that he was just acting.

"Nothing," Lizzie snarled, shoving another overflowing punch cup at a dancer.

"I think you don't want my help because you're scared. What if you find out I'm not such a bad guy?" Tommy smiled challengingly, looking like an all-American stud.

"I thought you said he was a dumb jock, Lizzie," Class Angel chirped. "That was quite insightful." It was ridiculously hot under the set lights, and Amelie felt like her thick layer of body glitter—a teen movie must if you were playing a diva or a supernatural being—was melting into her pores.

Lizzie slammed the ladle into the punch bowl, sending orange liquid flying at an extra in a white strapless dress. "Would you leave me alone?"

"Fine." Tommy stomped off, thinking Lizzie was talking to him, not her invisible angel.

"And cut," the AD hollered.

"Perfect," Dirk, the director, mumbled, barely looking up from his clipboard.

Kady high-fived Hunter and Amelie. "It's freaky trying to play off of both of you without a group dynamic." She wriggled out of her hoodie, sticking her tongue out in feigned fatigue. "I'm overheating—be right back." Kady hustled off toward the craft services table, her character's Chuck Taylors almost silent on the wood floor.

Amelie spun on her heel, happy to see Hunter still standing there.

"Hey," he said, his dark eyes twinkling beneath the hot overhead lights. "It's so good to see you."

He enveloped her in a hug. He smelled fresh, like Downy fabric softener and soap. Despite the wings on her back, some very unangelic thoughts popped into Amelie's brain.

Hunter let her go and held her at arm's length. "It's weird not to be able to look at you while we're filming," he commented, and Amelie's heart beat heart-attack fast. "You look so different."

Was he noticing that she'd grown? Um, everywhere? She was taller, with long, athletic legs. Her chubby little-kid cheeks had thinned out, making her lips look fuller. She'd had her teeth straightened with Invisalign braces, and her slight overbite had vanished. Most importantly, she wore a B-cup.

"I know," Amelie said, wishing her voice sounded a little more Scarlett Johansson and less Minnie Mouse. She shrugged, the strap of her white Juicy Couture tank falling off her shoulder. Even though she was playing an angel, at least she got to dress like a teenager. Well, a teen-ager with wings. She was enjoying her modern costume, free of frills and princessy poufs. She looked up at him with what she hoped was a seductive gaze.

"It's just so cool, you know, finally getting to work together again," Hunter said, his hand still folded warmly around hers. "You're half the reason I took the movie at the last minute."

If the nylon wings strapped to Amelie's back had been real, she would have been hovering six feet off the ground right now. She tucked a stray strand of red hair behind her ear. "Aww, thanks. That's sweet."

"Come on, you taught me everything I know. At age eleven," Hunter teased, with a flirty wink.

Amelie's skin prickled in excitement. She could almost hear the collective disappointed sigh of the eight million girls who'd prayed for Hunter Sparks to look at them the way he was looking at Amelie right now.

You're the reason I took the movie. So all these years,

Hunter had been waiting for his chance to see her again, too?

"So what are you up to tonight?" Amelie asked boldly. "Is it Baskin-Robbins time yet?" She raised an eyebrow. Back when they'd first worked together, they'd gone for sundaes together at least once a week.

"Actually, I—" Hunter began, but he was interrupted by the reappearance of Kady, a cold bottle of Fiji water in hand and the front of her tank top tied into a knot above her belly button. Several young male production assistants, arms laden with Starbucks trays, slowed to stare at Kady's tanned midriff, accentuated by a Swarovski-crystal star-shaped navel ring.

Hunter high-fived her. "Parker. Friday night killed. The Standard's so much better than when it first opened."

Kady shrugged nonchalantly. "Told you."

Amelie felt like she'd been clocked over the head with a giant sign that read, LOSER! The Standard. The invitation Amelie had declined after the *A-List* party . . . to go home with her mom. Hunter had been there? Of course he'd been there. Did she think everyone was like her, constantly worried about doing the wrong thing?

"You headed to Hyde again tonight?" Hunter now fixed his dark eyes on Kady.

She nodded. "Me. The twins. A few others. Just call me the social committee."

"Sweet." Hunter grinned. "I wanted to drop in at Social really quick, see if Lindsay and Danny and those guys are there. That cool?"

Kady rolled her eyes at Amelie, as though Hunter

wouldn't know Hollywood from Vine if it weren't for her expertise. "Yeah, that's cool."

"Nice," Hunter said, running a hand over his short hair before turning back to Amelie. "See ya, li'l sis." He gave her another hug. It couldn't have been more brotherly if they were Baldwins.

Slinging an arm casually over Kady's shoulder, Hunter strolled off.

Amelie watched them walk away, Kady's head casually nestled in the crook of Hunter's arm. She felt like her white outfit was turning green with envy, and turned around to stop torturing herself.

Li'l sis. So that was it. Hunter did love her . . . like a little sister.

Someone tapped her on the shoulder. Amelie turned, hoping it was Hunter, having changed his mind. Instead, Gary slouched in front of her, his ball cap in his hands.

"Amelie, you can get going now," he said. "We're going to wrap up the dance shots now, and we don't need you."

Amelie nodded glumly, turning on her white Lanvin flats to walk—alone—back to her trailer.

He was right. Who needed a little sister getting in the way of the big kids' fun?

PLEASED TO MEET YOU

Monday morning, Jojo stared out the tinted window of Barbar's bodyguards' Escalade, her whole body alive with nervous excitement. Outside, rows of palm trees and sixteen-foot hedges shielded stars' homes from view. It was hard to believe she was living in one now. The best one, no less.

After a lengthy long-distance call with her dads last night, they'd all agreed it was best for Jojo to stay in Beverly Hills. It turned out that Barkley and Lailah had proposed the idea to her dads before Jojo had even come to L.A. Fred and Bradley admitted that when they left her at the Sacramento airport, they'd had a feeling it was a real goodbye. "Our place here isn't exactly a teenage girl's dream," Fred had said, trying to laugh but sounding a little rueful. "Don't worry about us," Bradley had chimed in, hearing the concern in Jojo's voice. "Think of this as our extended honeymoon." As she hung up the phone, Jojo had felt sad. But this morning, as the sun rose higher over Beverly Hills, excitement had overtaken her.

Just twelve hours ago, she'd thought she was headed to icy Greenland; now, she was headed to Beverly Hills

High. *The* Beverly Hills High, where Tori Spelling, Alicia Silverstone, and Angelina Jolie had spent their teenage years. She was sitting in the back of a sleek black Escalade with Myla, who was listening to Kanye and scribbling in a black Moleskine notebook. Myla wore cream Maison Martin Margiela knee-high boots with a supershort L.A.M.B. plaid mini and a white Zac Posen blouse that tied at the neck. All her school gear was tucked into an oversize red Dior hobo.

Jojo told herself not to stare, even though her new sister was even more gorgeous in person than in photographs. Myla had felt sick yesterday and spent the better part of the day in her room. She looked pretty great now, though, and Jojo couldn't wait till she was 100 percent. In last month's *Seventeen* poll, "What celeb would you like to go shopping with?" Myla had won 79 percent of the vote—including Jojo's. Jojo couldn't believe that soon enough she'd actually get to do it.

The driver turned from Beverly Glen onto Santa Monica Boulevard. Jojo watched men and women in suits head into Century City's chrome-and-glass office buildings. They passed a Coffee Bean, and when the driver turned again, Jojo almost gasped. Set back from Moreno Drive, Beverly Hills High's pristine white buildings practically gleamed in the sun. A vast expanse of lush green lawn spread out before the school.

Graceful girls in *Vogue*-caliber outfits stepped out of dark town cars, checking BlackBerries and iPhones as they went. Tanned guys with artfully messy surfer hair high-fived their friends. Preppy, wannabe-agent types sat on the stair railings, sizing up the female student body like they were scouting talent. It was so different from JFK High in Sacramento, a '70s-looking building surrounded by strips of patchy lawn and a cracked gray parking lot. Jojo clenched every muscle in her body to stop herself from hurtling out the door and spinning *Sound of Music* style on BHH's front lawn.

The car came to a stop and Myla gracefully extracted herself from the vehicle. Jojo hopped out next. No sooner had her Steve Madden flats hit the asphalt than a crowd of photographers appeared, surrounding the two girls like hyenas around their prey. Jojo gasped, wondering how she'd failed to notice so many telephoto lenses. Just seconds before, all of the paps had looked like slightly shabby pedestrians or parents taking their kids to school.

Cameras fired in a symphony of clicks, whirs, and dings, as questions came at them rapid-fire.

"Jojo, what's it like finding out you're Barbar's daughter? And Myla's sister?"

"Jojo, is it true you were raised by two men? And how do they feel about this?"

"Myla, how are you handling your parents having a real, biological child? Are you jealous?"

"Come on, guys. Stop causing trouble," Myla scoffed, almost flirtatiously. She coolly fluffed her hair, her perfect berry-stained pout growing into a wide smile. "What girl wouldn't want a sister her age? It's going to be like one big sleepover."

Myla reached to clutch Jojo's arm. She pulled her in close, and Jojo was engulfed in Myla's Chanel Chance perfume.

Jojo relaxed into Myla's grip as the paparazzi eagerly snapped shots of the sisters side by side. She was glad Myla was here, because she would have been completely paralyzed facing the photogs on her own.

"Jojo, is that true?" A pudgy guy in a stained and faded Team Aniston tee pushed a handheld video camera near Jojo's face, his fishlike eyes probing her.

Jojo laughed nervously. "I'm still getting used to everything. But I feel so lucky to be here, and to finally have met my parents." She smiled at Myla, who grinned right back. "And my sister, too."

Suddenly she pictured kids at JFK High, passing around the *Us Weekly* with her and Myla on the cover. It would fall into Justin Klatch's hands, and he'd stare at Jojo's glossy face, regretting that he'd missed his chance with her and wondering if he'd ever see her again. The thought made Jojo smile.

The cameras fired away. The pudgy guy squinted his eyes at Jojo again. "Are you nervous about starting Beverly Hills High?"

Jojo frowned. Why should she be nervous? It looked like a country club. But before she could answer, Myla pulled her protectively through an opening between two of the photographers.

"That's enough, guys, we're on school grounds," Myla cooed. "You know the rules. And you got enough for one day. Show's over." She smiled demurely, giving them a wave that was part friendly, part "do what I say *now*." Amazingly, the photographers instantly departed. Jojo stared at Myla with awe.

Myla let go of Jojo and rehitched her hobo bag on her

shoulder. She strode toward the doors of the school, and Jojo followed.

"That was insane," Jojo said, her North Face backpack slapping against her shoulder blade. Willa had overnighted some of Jojo's things from Sacramento, and along with her usual school bag, she wore a pair of gray pin-striped trousers from H&M, her silver Steve Madden flats, and a red Gap V-neck. "I guess I need to practice my 'no pictures, please!' pose. And I have to get some giant sunglasses. How did they even know we were coming? Lailah—I mean Mom—just enrolled me this morning!"

Without answering, Myla headed purposefully toward a set of trees lining the front of the school. The other students seemed to clear a path for Myla as she walked by, like Moses parting the Red Sea. Jojo felt proud to be walking beside her. *That's right, we're Barbar's kids,* Jojo thought. *Me and my sister.*

Finally Myla slowed, reaching three girls who stood in the shade of the library building. The bobbed brunette in the center dropped her BlackBerry into her royal blue tote and shrieked gleefully at Myla's approach. She wore olive-colored Lanvin platform gladiator sandals with a sleeveless Marc Jacobs peony-print dress.

The girls on either side, one with impossibly long legs and long blond waves, the other with buttery hair pulled in a high ponytail, gave excited two-handed waves, their handbags—a yellow Kooba tote and a black patent Miu Miu shopper, respectively—swinging rapidly. They each took a step forward, planting air kisses on Myla's bronzed cheeks.

"Thank God you're back," the brunette said. "We have so much catching up to do, Miss Save-the-World."

"You look hot," the ponytailed girl put in, clearly comparing her pleated Nina Ricci skirt to Myla's plaid number. The long-legged blonde nodded enthusiastically, her sapphire earrings swinging.

"Billie, Talia, Fortune. I missed you guys," Myla said blithely.

The trio paused and looked toward Jojo, who suddenly felt like she was wearing sewn-together toilet seat covers.

Then the brunette—Talia, it must have been—widened her eyes. "Oh my God," she said, understanding washing over her face. "I just got the TMZ blast. You're Myla's new—"

"She's nobody," Myla snapped, checking her mile-long eyelashes in the mirror of her Chanel compact. She closed it with a click, and Jojo's stomach tightened. *Huh?*

Talia leapt back as though Myla had just announced Jojo's battle with leprosy.

Myla eyed Jojo's flats. "I hope those shoes are comfortable," she said coolly. "Because if you don't meet me out front at three sharp, you'll be walking home in them."

At that, Myla, Billie, Talia, and Fortune turned toward the foyer of Beverly Hills High and walked away.

Jojo stood there stupidly, feeling like she'd been punched in the gut. Myla wasn't excited to have a sister her age, and it was *not* going to be one big sleepover. She was faking it for the paparazzi and wanted nothing to do with Jojo.

She watched as a set of caramel-haired twins—whom she recognized from the *School of Scandal* billboards—scuttled up to Myla. Myla muttered something to them, and the three girls looked in Jojo's direction and laughed.

Jojo felt like she was having an out-of-body experience, watching herself look out on the green lawn that had seemed so promising minutes before. A group of girls clad in head-to-toe pink looked Jojo over, their glossy lips curled in haughty sneers. Guys in red-and-black BHH hoodies passed Jojo with curious stares. Even a trio of *Babylon 5* T-shirt-wearing nerds looked down at their shoes as they dragged their bulging backpacks past her.

Right now, Willa was probably with the rest of the girls' soccer team, trash-talking-slash-flirting with the boys' team about the Battle of the Sexes game scheduled for Spirit Week. And Jojo . . . was completely alone.

Not to mention wearing BHH's official REJECT stamp on her forehead. Courtesy of her dear sister.

JANE DOE

Jacob Porter-Goldsmith—no, Jake—fought back a sigh as he yanked open the door to the Beverly Hills High tutoring office after school.

"Yo, PG," bellowed the familiar voice of Rod Stegerson, a senior football player, behind him. Jake turned and caught a balled-up piece of paper as it flew at his head. Good reflexes aside, today hadn't gone at all how he'd planned. Jake was, as Rod had just affirmed, still PG. Okay, so Molly Marcheesi from advanced calc had practically hyperventilated at the sight of his math camp folder. Unfortunately, girls who wore *I Heart Parabolas* T-shirts weren't the kind he was hoping to get all hot and bothered. He wanted the Mylas and Minas and girls with other sexy and impossible names to check out his hip, out-of-control hair, to notice the way his green athletic-cut tee brought out the flecks of green in his hazel eyes. What more bait did he need?

Entering the tutoring office, he noticed the cute student aide manning the desk. She was tiny, with wavy dishwater blond hair.

He mustered his coolest "what's up?" nod, and the

cute girl half-smiled. *All right.* Better. He approached the counter, half leaning on it so that his biceps looked bigger.

"Hi," he finally said, dismissing all the funny lines in his head as lame. "I'm Jake."

The girl stood up. "Kate." She smiled, a full-on encouraging smile. Her eyes were brown and she wore a big heart medallion that dipped into the V of her thin white cotton T-shirt.

"Jacob Porter-Goldsmith, as I live and breathe." The nasally voice of Phyllis Steinman, the ancient tutoring office secretary, cut in. She appeared beside Kate from the adjoining office. "My God, when'd you grow so much? What on earth were they feeding you at that math camp?"

Jake's stomach tightened. Phyllis attended his father's synagogue and therefore treated Jake like a long-lost nephew.

"Kate, you should have seen him last year, all skin and bone and so awkward, let me tell you," Phyllis continued, placing a knotted hand on Kate's shoulder. Kate instantly shifted her eyes away from him and nodded politely at Phyllis.

"Now he's a—what do you kids say? A hunk." She beamed. "A hunk!"

Jake prayed for an earthquake so he'd have an excuse to run.

"And he's a real catch!" Phyllis skittered behind the counter, opening a file cabinet. "A math tutor. A real brain. And he's never had a girlfriend. I still need him to meet my niece Shana."

Kate nodded again, and began restacking the file folders spread on her desk, lingering over a copy of the cafeteria menu like it contained must-read school gossip.

Jake stood wordlessly as Phyllis continued her search. He read every motivational poster in the room, willing himself not to turn red with embarrassment, and to "hang in there," like the little white kitten suspended from a clothesline. Finally, Phyllis produced Jake's folder and slid it to him. "Here you go, *bubbeleh*, your tutoring assignment." She winked. "Go get 'em, tiger."

"Thanks, Mrs. Steinman," he said, taking the file and backing out of the office. Kate didn't so much as look up.

Jake waited until he was safely in the Corolla to open his file. He had to meet his tutee, Jane Doe, in Culver City in forty-five minutes. He looked again at the name printed in twelve-point Courier font. Jane Doe? Weird.

When Jake approached the address on his tutor sheet, he almost called to see if there'd been a mistake. The only thing around for blocks on this stretch of Venice Boulevard was Transnational Pictures. He pulled into the main drive, stopping at the security hut. A gruff-looking guy in his mid-forties turned on his stool, looking down at Jake. "Name and who you're here to see," he said boredly.

"Sorry, man," Jake said, handing him his papers. "I'm a tutor and I'm wondering if maybe I'm reading this address wrong."

"We get lots of tutors." The guard's name tag read ED. He checked Jake's paper and grabbed an adhesive badge off the desk. JACOB PORTER-GOLDSMITH was printed beneath the Transnational logo. "You're going to follow Jackson

Sharpe Drive all the way to the end. Look for Soundstage 8 and park on the east end. One of the crew will take you to the trailer."

Ah, Jake thought. Kid star, he should have known. That explained the "Jane Doe." It was probably Abigail Breslin, or one of the Fanning sisters, who sort of creeped Jake out. Kid actors were known to be tutoring nightmares—often they were too young to have personal assistants, so they treated their tutors like servants. His friend Miles had tutored an eleven-year-old actor from *Hannah Montana* in biology last year, and the kid had made Miles get him decaf, extra-foam lattes, pick up his dry cleaning, and plan dates for him and his twelve-year-old girlfriend.

"Thanks." Jake took the badge and slowly steered the Corolla down the drive, abutted on both sides by Transnational soundstages. Construction crews were packing up for the day, pulling the giant sliding doors closed. He caught a glimpse of a giant moon-rock formation, activating his Nerd Alert, but pushed curiosity from his mind.

At Soundstage 8, he pulled in behind an old Thunderbird convertible. Five identical trailers were lined up in a parking lot across Ben Hur Boulevard. He got out of the car, looking around to see if the promised crew person would lead him to the right trailer. No one was in sight.

He sighed, reaching in for his worksheets, flash cards, and Sum of Us guide. From the cupholder, he grabbed the half-empty Starbucks he'd drunk on the way to school that morning. Hands now full, Jake turned and crashed directly into something. Someone. A guy about a head taller than him. The cold latte exploded all over the front of his shirt.

"Oh, man, I'm sorry," the big guy said, grabbing Jacob's stack of papers and producing a grimy rag from his back pocket.

Jake dabbed fruitlessly at his soaked shirt. "It's no big deal," he said. "I have another shirt."

He did have another shirt. A shirt from math camp. Complete with a Star of David and the words *Everyone Loves a Math Mensch*. It wasn't exactly stylish, but it was better than a huge coffee stain.

Jake took the shirt from his trunk and pulled off the soaked green tee. "You're the tutor, right?" the guy asked. Jake nodded as he pulled the fresh shirt over his head. At least it smelled clean. "Second trailer from the left. She's expecting you."

Jake sighed, making his way to the door of the trailer. He knocked and stood there for a few seconds, feeling like a creepy stalker, even though he didn't know who he was stalking. Finally, the door opened. It took him a second to realize he was face-to-face with Fairy Princess.

Make that Amelie Adams, wearing skimpy red cotton gym shorts that clung to her curves and a tight white tank top. She blew back a strand of fiery hair that fell from a loose ponytail at the nape of her neck. As Fairy Princess she was cute, like a girl next door who really liked playing dress-up. But as regular Amelie, in the door of her trailer, wearing very little . . . she was just plain hot.

He held a hand out for Amelie to shake, holding his folders and study materials over the Star of David on his T-shirt. "I'm Jake Porter-Goldsmith, with Sum of Us," he said, deciding to be all business. It was better than trying to be funny and failing.

"I'm Amelie Adams," she said, her small hand folding around his. She stepped back from the door into her minimalist trailer. In the center of the floor was a daisy-print yoga mat, and near the other end, two chairs were tucked into a small round table piled high with novels and scripts. "Sorry about the mess," she said sheepishly. "I was just going through some stuff my agent sent over." She hefted the pile of books and papers from the table to the floor, gesturing for Jake to sit.

He had no choice but to put his tutoring materials on the table, revealing the full nerd quotient of his outfit. Amelie retrieved bottles of Fiji water from a Styrofoam cooler and placed them in the center of the table. "The fridge conked out today," she explained, gesturing to the small kitchenette. She sat across from him, her blue eyes falling on his shirt. She giggled. *Great*, Jacob thought, nervously twisting open his water. *She's laughing at me already*.

"Cool shirt," she said, reaching across the table to read the *Math Mensch* slogan in full. "I haven't seen that one yet."

"It's, um, I got it this summer." Jake didn't think he'd ever been this close to a girl before. At least not one this beautiful. Amelie could easily play Red Sonja—a crappy comic, but it featured a hot chick. Jake hid it between his copies of *Hellboy* and *Sandman*.

She let go, her face forming a frown. "I guess it's been a while since I hit Fred Segal."

Fred Segal? That was where all the kids with black

Amex cards bought their two-hundred-dollar jeans and ninety-dollar . . . *T-shirts*. *Ohhh*. Amelie Adams thought the shirt was *ironic*. And that he was cool enough to shop there. Jake felt relief wash over him.

"I guess so," he managed, flipping open his binder of geometry exercises. "Why don't we get started?" he said coolly—like sitting across from a superstarlet was just another day in the life of Jacob, make that Jake, Porter-Goldsmith.

WHAT'S MINE IS MINE

"So you're really, truly over?" Talia Montgomery looked sideways at Myla from her perch on the wall surrounding the Beverly Hills High courtyard. Magnolia trees cast shady relief from the warm late afternoon sun, and a breeze off the Pacific wafted through the open area, spreading the scent of red-and-white Double Delight roses from a garden planted as a gift from the class of '02. Talia cocked her head expectantly, her dark Katie Holmes–circa '07 bob fanning over her lightly freckled skin.

Myla paced in front of her, the heels of her soft cream boots clicking against the courtyard's brick paving stones. It was Monday after school, and their entire clique of girlfriends was eyeing her expectantly. Finally she nodded, clutching her Moleskine primly to her chest.

"Does this mean I won't be your maid of honor anymore?" Talia's glossy lips turned downwards in a practiced frown. She'd been planning Myla's wedding for a year.

Myla scowled at her best friend. Talia's dark hair had picked up some brassiness from the summer sun, Myla noticed. She needed some lowlights, and maybe a trim. Myla would tell her later on, in private. "Just because there's no Ash doesn't mean I'll never get married."

"You never know—new guy, new friends," piped up Fortune Weathers. She flicked her ponytail, which was curled like she was headed for a '50s sock hop. She was Talia's next-door neighbor and competed with Talia for everything, most of all Myla's friendship. Fortune's parents traveled a lot, to find unique clothing and houseware lines for their five international boutiques, Weathers or Not. They rarely minded if Fortune had friends over while they were away, even if "friends" meant half of BHH's student body. The good half.

"Are you sure you guys won't make up?" squeaked Billie Bollman, an all-legs blond with a perfect GPA but no common sense. Billie shook her long, shiny locks, the champagne waves tumbling over her last-season Theory jumper. Her father's company was responsible for one of downtown's only successful condominium developments, and Billie had inherited some of her dad's cautiousness when it came to money.

"Not a chance," Myla said, even though she knew it was only a matter of time before Ash came to his senses.

Now if only she could do something about Jojo. This morning, her parents had practically spoon-fed Jojo breakfast while Myla barely got a "good morning." Faking a stomach bug, she'd even gone to bed early the night before. Barkley and Lailah had only checked on her *once*. And then there was Jojo herself. Myla had seen the hopeful glint in Jojo's eye when she thought she was about to be introduced to Talia, Billie, and Fortune this morning. Wasn't it enough that she was the shiny new apple of their parents' eye? Myla didn't feel like sharing her friends, too. And she didn't have time to make nice with Jojo. She had, however, taken a few minutes to begin several choice rumors about her new sister. Everyone else had to deal with Advanced Gossip as a BHH graduation requirement, so why not Jojo? Hopefully she'd go Sacramental and leave.

With her work done on the Jojo front, Myla was now concentrating on more important affairs: pushing forward with her and Ash's "breakup" so he'd eventually see how serious this was, and ask for her forgiveness. Earlier today, she'd told him they needed to divide their assets: their friends. For their first two years at BHH, Myla and Ash's reign as golden couple had meant that they'd collected a circle of friends best described as "anyone who was anyone." Their group included children of top-tier actors, actresses, directors; the sons and daughters of the West Side's best agents, talent managers, producers, and executives; and basically anyone else with a good gene pool and the financial wherewithal to run up an all-night bottle service tab at Bar Marmont.

Now it was time to split them down the middle. Myla was nothing if not fair.

Of course, Ash was late. And Myla was getting annoyed. Their pseudo-breakup arrangement wasn't going according to her plan. She'd expected new groups to form with mixes of guys and girls. But instead, she just saw the makings of a classic boys-versus-girls battle, like kindergartners at recess. On her side of the courtyard were Talia, Fortune, Billie, and the Lacey twins, Moira and Deven—whose egos alone could have filled the Hollywood Bowl since they'd landed parts on *School of Scandal*. On the other side of the courtyard, lazing around like a photo spread for *Men's Vogue*, a cluster of BHH guys awaited Ash's arrival, hunched and posed in expensive nonchalance.

In her Moleskine, she'd listed some of the male student body she wanted to claim in her and Ash's "divorce." But Dirk Sommerfeld, Julius Grand, and Simon Todd were all huddled on *Ash's* side, not even paying her any attention.

Myla cat-stretched sexily in her short plaid skirt and tall boots. She hoped Ash's lame burnout buddies, like that horndog Geoff Schaffer and girl-crazy Tucker Swanson, would take a good long look and inform Ash of all he was missing.

She started to reach for her gold chain, the Green Lantern ring hidden beneath her blouse, before she caught herself. She didn't want Ash to know she still had it on, and she couldn't let her troops know she held out hope, either. She turned to the cluster of girls around her, all of whom stared at her expectantly.

"Okay, let's get started," Myla said, walking down the row of girls. "As you all know, the days of Myla and Ash are O-V-E-R."

"Over!" Billie exclaimed, looking teary-eyed. "That's so permanent."

Myla smiled patiently at her and continued, clutching her notebook to her chest as she paced in front of the girls. "I hope you all know what this means," she continued, her voice powerful. "Take one last look at the bonehead parade over there."

Myla pointed carelessly toward the group of mostly covetable guys on the other side of the courtyard. "We're done with them," she said. "Ash and I have split, and this is how the line has been drawn. Those burnouts, losers, pathetic nothings—they won't plague you any longer. As of today, they're dead to you."

Talia gasped. "But Mark got so cute over the summer," she whined, glancing over at Mark Bauman, who had finally stopped wearing vintage clothes this year and did smell a lot better.

"Enough of that, Talia," Myla snapped, feeling less sure of herself. Where was the loyalty?

Billie spoke up. "But what about social events? Geoff has the best parties. We can't be expected to miss those."

Myla focused her most withering stare on Billie. "You *can* be expected to miss those. Really, we're talking junior boys here."

Moira Lacey raised her hand haughtily. "So what are we going to do without boys? Become nuns?" she asked, a sneer on her recently improved face. Moira and her twin sister, Deven, had had a hard time landing roles in even school plays until a famous plastic surgeon repaired both girls' "deviated septums." A few snips, one CW show, standing color appointments at Fekkai, and suddenly they could question Myla Everhart?

Myla's stomach clenched as she took in her friends' dubious expressions. Even Talia, who was usually loyal to a fault, squinted skeptically. What *would* they do without boys? Make slice-and-bake cookies and watch *High School Musical* together?

She turned to look at the boys on the other side of the courtyard. Ash had finally made it, and each of his friends—scuzzy Geoff and that moron Tucker—gave a cheer and clapped Ash on the back like he'd just returned from battle. Probably congratulating him on nailing Cassie Eastman, like that was a real *accomplishment*. She wondered how long it would be before she could hold Ash's callused musician's hand again, or push his cowlicks off his face to see those hopeful, loving eyes. It couldn't be long, could it? This wasn't for real. It wasn't.

She turned back to her new subjects, lengthening her spine in her most regal posture.

"No one said there'd be no boys," she assured them, shifting her steely gaze from Billie to Talia to Deven and Moira, who wore identical sour expressions under their matching curtains of caramel hair. "Just not *those* boys."

The girls nodded, not entirely convinced but not about to challenge her.

"I for one think this is an ideal situation," Fortune asserted, her nose practically turning brown. "Myla knows what's she's doing. She landed Ash, didn't she? I bet by midterms, she'll have us all hooked up with hot college guys. Isn't that right, Myla?"

Myla resisted the urge to push Fortune off the wall. It was one thing for her to kiss ass and quite another for her to make empty promises to Myla's friends. Still, the other girls nodded, albeit halfheartedly. Myla sighed, wishing her supposed allies could muster half the energy that Ash was getting from his meathead friends across the way. But no queen kept her throne by giving her subjects free rein. She was a leader. And a good leader had to get used to being feared rather than loved. Right?

"Dude, I was down in Venice yesterday and these hot chicks from the coffee shop on Abbott-Kinney were, like, all over me. This little blonde is so perfect for you, Gilmour."

Geoff was practically pulling out his stringy dark hair with excitement over Ash's newly single status. He and Myla hadn't exactly gotten along, mostly because Geoff had once "borrowed" Barkley's medical marijuana card and then lost it. It was stupid, but Geoff hadn't meant anything by it. Girls who liked a project always went for Geoff, hoping to find the Jake Gyllenhaal beneath the grease.

Ash nodded, looking over Geoff's shoulder across the courtyard. Myla paced back and forth in front of her girlfriends in her cute plaid skirt and boots. She looked like a super-hot military general, rallying her troops. He wondered how long she'd torture him like this. A meeting to split their friends? Did she really think he didn't see through this? Myla wanted to scare him a little, so he'd come running back. But their fight this weekend had been *her* fault. Yeah, maybe he'd been being whiny, but she didn't have to pull out the bitch card.

"Dude, are you even listening?" Geoff practically barked at him. Ash recoiled from his friend's pungent breath. Geoff had had too many of the cafeteria's garlic fries.

"Yeah, man, chicks in Hermosa, right?" Ash pushed back his hair, trying to discern what Myla and her friends were discussing.

Tucker Swanson showed up on Ash's other side, punching him hard in the arm. "Venice, bro," Tucker said, nodding the "there be hot chicks" nod. "But we can score in Hermosa, too, for sure." He ran a hand over his freshly shaved head, covered in white-blond fuzz. He always got a drastic cut at the start of the school year and let it grow back to shoulder length over the next twelve months. Girls loved it, almost as much as they dug Tucker's lean surfer's physique—which he showed off by purchasing all of his tees at least a size too small.

Ash was surprised Tucker was even still around. Word was Zuma had some great waves today, and Tucker tried to hit the best surf before and after school. At least, when he and Ash weren't meeting at Ash's house or Tucker's garage to try getting a band going. Tucker's dad, who used the stage name Dell Pearl, had been a pretty huge pop star in the '70s, famous for a song "Dear Amy," about Jimmy Carter's daughter. Tucker's plans for what kind of band he wanted to start all depended on the girl he was chasing at the moment. He fell in love with someone new every day.

"Dude, by the way, have you seen Myla's sister?" he whispered to Ash.

Ash hadn't seen the infamous Jojo yet, but he'd heard buzz about her in the halls. He briefly wondered how Myla was holding up: New siblings always sank her into a self-pitying "I'm so alone" mood. Not that she was ever alone, with her collection of free-trade siblings and the ever-present Fashionista Task Force. If anything, Jojo was probably the one feeling lonely. But Ash was too wrapped up in his own problems to haul out the Welcome Wagon for a new girl, even if she was Myla's sister.

"She looks so nice, you know? Plus, you already know she's got a hot mom. Bo-nus," Tucker continued, grinning lasciviously and dancing from side to side in his Havaianas.

Ash shrugged him off. Tucker was a dog sometimes, but he was also Ash's oldest friend—if you didn't count Jacob Porter-Goldsmith. They'd been friends growing up, but had stopped hanging out when Ash got cool and Jake got . . . well, not. Now they exchanged the briefest of nods if they both happened to be in their front yards at the same time.

"You're free again, player!" Julius Grand practically howled. He tacked on a wolf whistle, at odds with his dapper argyle sweater vest. Myla always said he classed up Ash's group.

Mark Bauman stepped forward to high-five Ash. Ash limply slapped his hand. Gone were Mark's trademark nasty-ass dreads that creeped Myla out. He now sported a Zac Efron haircut that made him look like a total douche, but word was he'd already gotten "digits" from four hot sophomores today. Mark's parents were big-shot environmentalists, and Mark—formerly a kind-of-shy kid in the ecology club—used that cred to scam chicks. He had played the "let's save the Earth . . . together in my Prius" card with many a naïve, dolphin-loving female. His eco-player persona was rounded out by his collection of hemp shirts and organic Levi's. "Wait until the chickees get a load of you," Mark said. "Ash Gilmour's on the *prowl*. We gotta take you to the Valley. Just the fact that you bagged Myla Everhart is enough to make girls in Burbank want to compete for your affections. Dude, I'll take your fucking leftovers!" Mark whooped loudly, making a humping motion with his hips like a wildebeest on *Animal Planet*. To Ash's friends, the only thing better than actually scoring with chicks was talking about it.

Ash knew Mark was right. Girls swarmed him just because of his high-powered father. It also didn't hurt that he had muscles and a tan from hours spent surfing, could play "Sympathy for the Devil" with his eyes closed, and drove a sweet vintage Camaro that he could smoothly whip around the curves of Mulholland Drive.

It was true: He could have had anyone he wanted. But he wanted Myla.

God, this was stupid. He couldn't wait until a week or a month from now, when he'd get to tease Myla about her first-day-of-school insanity. They could name it, like, Fake Breakup Day. He snuck a glance at her. She was twenty feet away, probably hearing from her friends how many guys were dying to go out with *her*. The thought hit him like a bad Baja Fresh taco. He briefly wondered how Myla would respond if he crossed the courtyard, grabbed her by the waist, and pulled her in for the kiss of her life. Maybe she'd love it. Probably she'd kick him right in the nuts with one of those wicked boots.

Ash just grinned weakly at Mark. "They're all yours," he said.

LOSERVILLE, POPULATION TWO

Amelie Adams, 16, is best known for her role as Kidz
Network's Fairy Princess. Acting since she was a toddler,
Adams got her start in a national Pampers campaign as a
spokesbaby for a new line of pull-up diapers.

Unlike some of her Hollywood peers, Adams isn't a
Hollywood club scene regular. She is most frequently pho-
tographed at Kidz Network events, or while shopping in
Beverly Hills with her mother and manager, Helen.

Currently, Amelie is playing the title role in the upcoming
teen comedy *Class Angel*. It is rumored she was considered
for the part of Emma Hardy in *The A-List*, but producers
thought her Fairy Princess past would cause fans not to take
her seriously in a such a mature role.

According to interviews, Amelie loves Meryl Streep
movies, the San Diego Zoo, and Mexican cuisine, especially carne asada tacos. Her favorite books include *Jane
Eyre*, the Harry Potter series, and *Bridget Jones's Diary*.

Jacob reread Amelie Adams' Wikipedia page for the
fourth time in fifteen minutes. He'd spent most of his
lunch period in the computer lab, absorbing everything
he could find out about Amelie Adams. He'd even been
to the Fairy Princess fan club page.

His tutoring session with Amelie yesterday had gone so well. She seemed genuinely interested in learning geometry, and she was easy to talk to. Jacob always felt like the girls at BHH were speaking another language, one that infinite studying couldn't help him to learn. Not that they talked to him much anyway.

He gazed at Amelie's head shot as he mentally recited what he'd learned about her from Wikipedia, the Internet Movie Database, and her fan club page: *Had one dog, a basset hound named Sylvio, until she was twelve; loves carne asada tacos; dream costars include Meryl Streep and Johnny Depp; first line on* Fairy Princess *was, "Bubblelemon, we need to fly to the Enchanted Forest right away!"*

He clicked to the official *Fairy Princess* show page. The theme song blared from the iMac's speakers, and he scrambled to find the volume control. "We can laugh and play all day / Charming the kingdom with our magical ways. / Let's all fly to Fragonia to make friends / With Fairy Princess!"

A feminine giggle rang out behind him.

Jacob clicked the mute button and turned around. A cute brunette with almost purple eyes was smirking at him.

Jojo slapped her hand over her mouth. She hadn't *meant* to laugh. With her luck, this cute guy was probably, like, senior class president or something. So maybe he had a Fairy Princess fetish, but now that she'd laughed at him, he'd ensure no one talked to her all school year. If Myla hadn't done that already.

Jojo had wandered into the computer lab after sitting in a corner of the modernly appointed cafeteria, picking at her whole-grain-mac-and-asiago-cheese, trying not to notice everyone staring at her. Myla had been holding court at a table populated by girls whose handbags alone could have bought Jojo the 2001 Ford Explorer she'd been coveting back in Sacramento. She'd heard titters from Myla's seatmates as she walked past to get a fork, and she knew why: Earlier today, two cheerleaders at a locker only five feet from Jojo had been discussing how "that Milford girl" had only come to live with Barbar to steal money to support her meth habit. Even the tables of kids who were obviously of second-tier social status—carrying last year's iPhones and wearing two-hundred-dollar, rather than four-hundred-dollar, jeans—had giggled and coughed non-subtle exclamations to one another when Jojo passed. She had distinctly heard the words *head lice*.

So now here she was, looking for an open computer so she could IM—make that Instant Misery—Willa with her woeful tales of being a BHH outcast on day two of school.

"It's not what it looks like," the cute guy said, his voice cracking. Despite his cool-guy curly hair and tightish blue tee, he was wearing a too-short pair of Old Navy carpenter-style jeans and brighter-than-bright white sneakers. In her Roxy hoodie and Bebe miniskirt—which would have crowned her fashion queen in Sacramento but apparently made her thoroughly Valley-esque here—she was actually beating this guy for style points. Maybe she didn't need to feel intimidated after all.

Jojo plopped down at the empty iMac next to him. He quickly clicked on another Firefox tab, hiding the evidence of his Fairy Princess fandom. Another Amelie Adams page popped up in its place.

"Sooo, you're into Fairy Princess?" Jojo smiled. She spun her chair so she was facing him.

He sighed and leaned back in his chair, like some CEO lazing in his corner office. "You've just met her number one fan."

Jojo laughed again. A guy who looked like a mini-lawyer shushed her from the row behind them.

The guy smiled. "Actually, I'm tutoring Amelie Adams in geometry."

Jojo whistled, impressed. "Nice gig," she said, stretching out a hand. "I'm Jojo Milford, the new girl."

"Ohhh," Jacob said, registering her lavender eyes. This wasn't just any cute brunette he was talking to, but Barbar's daughter. Miles had recounted in detail seeing Jojo and Myla facing down a paparazzi attack before school, describing Jojo's wide, deep-set eyes as "sci-fi, anime-girl hot." For once, Miles hadn't been far off the mark. "I've heard about you," he said with a polite nod.

Jojo bit her lip. Was her entire *body* covered in Myla's REJECT stamp? "That stuff—it's not true. At all," Jojo mumbled.

The guy shrugged. "I just heard you were Barbar's daughter. Myla's sister."

"Oh," Jojo said, blushing. Of course she'd assumed the worst. "Well . . . people are saying things. I guess I should've expected it, being suddenly famous or whatever," she said, looking down at the diamond-patterned carpet. It wasn't like her to be opening up to someone she'd only just met, but it actually didn't feel weird at all. Then again, stranger things had happened over the last few days. "I feel like everyone's staring at me, and every new rumor is way worse than the last one. I'm just . . . embarrassed. And I really don't have head lice." She smiled weakly.

The guy ran a hand through his messy curls. "It's better than being invisible, believe me. I mean, the talk, not the head lice." He chuckled, his hazel eyes smiling. "And, no offense, but this is BHH. Everyone here is sort of famous. Today it's you, but don't worry—by the end of the week, they'll have moved onto something, or someone, else."

The guy shook her hand. "By the way, I'm Jake Porter-Goldsmith." He grinned dorkily. "Fairy Princess lover and proud of it. But, really, don't tell anyone. This school makes Shark Week look like Disneyland."

Jojo raised her eyebrows. She hoped Jake Porter-Goldsmith was right. If so, she couldn't help but feel a little sorry for BHH's next victim.

HOBOS WITH BALENCIAGAS

Later that afternoon, Jojo sat with Lailah and Myla near the far edge of the pool, where miniature palm trees gave way to an actual waterfall. Sunlight bounced off the pool's aquamarine surface, and she breathed in the sweet aromas of orange blossoms and star jasmine. Lailah was stretched out on a lounge, an array of sunscreens assembled on the teak table next to her. She wore a black Versace string bikini that showcased a figure Jojo prayed to inherit and a wide-brimmed sun hat, to protect her cream-colored skin from the sun. Myla fidgeted in an overstuffed Brown Jordan patio chair on Lailah's other side.

On an open expanse of the backyard next to the pool, Barkley was playing Wiffle ball with Mahalo, Bobby, and Nelson. Ajani and Indigo squealed with delight in the sandbox as they poured a bucket of sand over a Hannah Montana doll's head.

Suddenly Myla sprang up, clomping across the pool tiles in her violet sandals. "Jojo, I'm going to call Lucy for a San Pellegrino with lemon." Her singsong tone echoed as she disappeared inside the cabana. "Do you want one?"

"Um, no, I think I'm okay," Jojo said, watching as Ajani shoved the Hannah doll's head into a miniature sand dune. "Thanks, though."

"I'll have her bring you one, just in case," Myla said in a dulcet tone that could have made woodland animals flock to her. *She'd probably just skewer them to make kebabs,* Jojo thought.

"Thanks," she said, not meaning it. The perfection of the moment—mother and daughters poolside beneath a blue sky striped with wispy white clouds—belied the thick tension between Myla and Jojo. Myla's Pollyanna act was just that, an act, for Lailah's benefit.

Jojo had spoken to her dads before school today, but hadn't had the heart to tell them that her fantastic first weekend had morphed into a hell-on-Earth week. They'd sounded so happy, telling her about Nuuk and its ice floes, and seemed relieved when she'd lied and said that BHH was treating her great so far. Maybe someday soon, she wouldn't have to lie.

After calling in their drink orders to Lucy, the Everharts' live-in housekeeper, Myla began digging around in the pool house, a Tahitian beach house slightly at odds with the majestic Everhart estate. The sound of cabinets banging shut wafted over to Jojo as Myla searched for items to fill her beach bag, getting ready for some kind of legendary pool party at the Beverly Hills Hotel. *She* hadn't shared this information with Jojo, of course—Jojo had overheard Billie Bollman and Fortune Weathers debating one-pieces versus bikinis in English class.

As Myla hunted for supplies, Lailah tilted her

unmistakable profile in Jojo's direction. "Jojo, is school going okay?"

Jojo nodded, faking a contented smile. "Yeah, great."

Lailah pulled down her Gucci sunglasses and studied Jojo intently. "Myla has been showing you around?"

Jojo half-shrugged. She could spill the full dish on Myla right here and now, if she wanted. But she was still too terrified of her malicious stepsister to risk pissing her off. If Myla was this mean when all Jojo had done was show up, she shuddered to think how the girl would retaliate to tattling. "Yeah, she kind of showed me what I'm in for," Jojo said instead, which wasn't a complete lie. "We're not in a lot of the same classes so, you know. . . ." Jojo trailed off.

A Wiffle ball from Bobby's home run landed next to Lailah. She grabbed the ball and threw it backwards, toward the boys. "Nice hit," she said, never taking her eyes off Jojo.

Myla emerged from the cabana, her silky wrap dress replaced with a Trina Turk petal pink and palm green tropical print cover-up that hit mid-thigh. She'd paired it with sky-high lime green Dior patent peep-toes. She casually slung a mint nylon Juicy Couture tote over her bare shoulder and plopped down on the chair on Jojo's other side.

At least Jojo was wearing a new Pucci her mom had given her this afternoon, a tropical print camisole dress splashed with aqua and lemon. For once she didn't feel like a pre-ball Cinderella next to a wickedly fashionable stepsister.

Lucy arrived with a tall glass of fizzy water, complete with a lime slice balanced on the rim.

"You must have met some people by now," Lailah pressed. "Maybe some of Myla's friends?"

Myla, her water glass poised at her lips, opened her mouth to say something.

"Well, I met this guy Jake in the computer lab," Jojo cut her off. She didn't have to tattle, but no way was she letting Myla pretend she'd welcomed Jojo into her exclusive inner sanctum. "Jake Porter-Goldsmith. He's really nice." Jojo smiled angelically at her mother before turning to flash a victorious grin at Myla.

Myla slipped on her Prada sunglasses, probably to roll her eyes behind them. She gulped her water, emptying the glass, and stood up, grabbing her bag.

Lailah looked past Jojo to Myla. "I'm sure Jojo would like to see the Beverly Hills Hotel." The comment was innocent enough, but there was an accusatory edge to her voice.

"Um, yeah," Myla said, only barely looking up from her lime green tote.

Jojo shook her head. "Oh, no, that's okay. I'm totally fine hanging here. Lucy's making quesadillas and me and the rest of the kids are watching *Spider-Man 2* tonight."

"It will be a good way for you to meet more of your classmates. I insist." Lailah got up from her lounger, wrapping a tropical print sarong around her waist. Barkley, mid-pitch to Mahalo, wolf-whistled at his wife. She beamed in his direction and removed her giant hat, her dark hair tumbling in waves to her shoulders.

Jojo felt a trickle of warm sweat slide down her back as every muscle in her body tensed. Lailah must have known what was going on with her daughters. But still, she was sending Jojo into the lion's den with the queen of the jungle.

Lailah hugged the girls and followed them all the way to the top of the winding driveway, where the hybrid SUV was waiting.

"Make sure Jojo has a good time," she instructed Myla once they were ensconced in the vehicle's backseat.

"Of course, Mom," Myla demurred. "She's my sister."

Myla glared at Jojo out of the corner of her eye. They were in the backseat of the Escalade, and Jojo had spent the entire ride admiring her new silver Hollywould wedges. Lailah had given the shoes to her this morning, claiming they'd come for her but "didn't fit." Lailah was always giving Jojo something. Yesterday, it had been a Dolce & Gabbana motorcycle jacket that Myla had been coveting for years. This morning, it was the silver wedges, and then after school the colorful Pucci sundress Jojo now wore.

Myla was getting really sick of her new sister's sweet-and-innocent act. Every time Jojo walked into a room, Lailah and Barkley stopped what they were doing to stare at their progeny. Barkley was so infatuated with his daughter that he'd made her his famous blueberry-and-chocolate-chip pancakes that morning, a recipe he hadn't broken out in a year. He'd even offered to drive her to school on his way to a meeting on the Fox lot—like they didn't have a driver for that.

Worst of all, *Myla* had come out by the pool first today, hoping for some alone time with her parents. She'd wanted to remind them that she was their first child, their main source of pride and joy. She'd hoped they'd finally ask her how Paris was, or praise her for her eloquent interview with *People* during their aid trip. That she'd finally get to tell them that she was going through the first romantic crisis of her young life—how could they not have noticed Ash was missing, when he usually ate dinner with them every night? But then Jojo had appeared, wearing the new Pucci and the silver sandals, and her parents positively beamed at their bio-kid. Myla had felt like one of her mom's Golden Globes, shoved in the china cabinet while Jojo, the Oscar, stood proudly in the foyer.

Jojo stared out the window at the light on Sunset and Crescent. A lady with frizzy blond hair wearing enormous sunglasses, an oversize *Knocked Up* T-shirt, and red Reebok high-tops watched her pocket-size dog poop in the grass lining the sidewalk. Jojo would have taken her for a hobo, had it not been for her glimmering gold Balenciaga bag.

Myla had been texting nonstop, brooding, the whole ride.

They pulled up to the majestic Beverly Hills Hotel. The building was a peachy shade of pink, and on one painted green facade facing the street, curvy script spelled out *Beverly Hills Hotel*. Jojo pictured Marilyn Monroe pulling up in a long white convertible. She'd bunked at the hotel's famed bungalows before, and Elizabeth Taylor had honeymooned with six of her eight husbands there.

Myla practically jumped onto the pavement, her skinny-heeled peep-toes clacking against the ground. She raced to the entrance, an overhead canopy painted with green and white stripes over a red carpet that led up to the hotel's main doors.

Jojo tried to savor the moment, the plush carpet cushioning every silver-wedged step. Her new Holly-woulds were quickly becoming her favorite shoes.

Inside, a massive art deco light fixture that looked like an upside-down feather duster cast a warm glow onto the thick palm leaf–print carpet. Low rose-hued armchairs formed a perfect circle, each aligned beneath glossy peach pillars the size of tree trunks. A harried-looking woman in a black business suit and reading glasses sat perusing the *New York Times* in one of the armchairs, her Samsonite luggage stacked neatly on a bellhop cart at her side. She glared at a snoring Eurotrash couple in tight black clothing sleeping in another chair.

Myla spun on her heels, facing Jojo. She reached into her bag and pulled out a champagne cork.

"Do you have your invitation?" She waved the cork slowly, allowing Jojo to see that the date, time, and BHH were inscribed in the cork's surface. Dropping it back in her bag, she sighed with faux sympathy. "This is a private party. Invite only. Guess you're not invited."

"Well, can't you do something?" Jojo bit her lip, feeling like an idiot. "I mean, this party can't be such a big deal that you couldn't at least get me through the door." She was trying to sound cool, but her voice bore a twinge of whininess. She knew her BHH classmates wouldn't exactly cheer at her arrival, but now that she was at the legendary hotel, Jojo felt desperate to see the pool—and to witness the party—even if she had to sit in a sun chair while everyone else went wild. Maybe while Myla wasn't looking, she'd even get the chance to talk to a few people and show them she wasn't a meth-addicted, head lice carrying, Amish-raised freak.

Myla rolled her eyes. "This party *is* a big deal. And yes, I could get you through the door. Easily. I just don't want to."

Jojo felt her face grow hot. "So what am I supposed to do?"

Myla grinned. "You can wait here in the lobby." She gestured to the empty armchairs. "Sit anywhere you like."

With that, she walked off in the direction of the pool, leaving Jojo standing there alone. Again.

Jojo sank into the nearest chair, smiling weakly at the *New York Times* lady, who barely looked up from her paper. She felt like Myla was burying her alive. Every time Jojo clawed her way near the surface, Myla was there with a shovel, ready to throw more dirt on her.

She pulled out her camera phone and snapped photos of her beautiful surroundings. Then, feeling ready to cry, she turned the lens on herself, taking a shot of her hangdog expression against the luxe background.

She punched in Willa's number and wrote a quick text.

Here I am, at the Beverly Hills Hotel, where everything happens. And I'm not part of any of it. Pretty glamorous, huh?

STALKERVILLE, POPULATION ONE

"God, all this time I thought a cosine was when two people agree to a contract." Amelie smiled self-consciously.

To her surprise, Jake registered her joke and laughed heartily. They were in her trailer, sitting at the tiny table.

"Wow, I need you around all the time to laugh at my bad jokes," Amelie said, flicking him lightly on the arm. She thought of earlier today, on set with Kady and Hunter. Amelie had asked how Hyde was the other night and tacked on, "Weird it's called Hyde, when everyone there wants to be seen." She'd even *winked*. Kady and Hunter had barely managed a forced half-chuckle between them. But being around Jake—it was nice. Easy. Sure they'd really only talked about math, but already she felt comfortable around him, like maybe they could be friends.

True, she didn't have a lot of friendship experiences to go by. Growing up in the business had earned her plenty of "friends" on her official Facebook and MySpace pages (with status updates and blogs carefully crafted by a thirty-something Kidz Network publicist). But real friends? She figured being part of an actual friendship *had* to feel something like she did right now: Like she could be silly or make a bad joke and her friend would either laugh hysterically or be honest and tease her about how lame the attempt was.

"So, um, what'd you get for problem ten?" Jake asked, trying to be professional. Amelie rolled her eyes, as if to say, *where's the fun in that?*, but obediently went back to her worksheet. As they talked through the next few problems, Jake had to force himself to focus. All he really wanted to do was gaze at Amelie's smiling blue eyes. He was still so amazed that she was smiling at *him*. Since they'd started their session an hour ago, Jake felt like every humiliation he'd suffered throughout high school for being a math whiz was entirely worth it. The time that Rod Stegerson had given him a wedgie in front of the junior high cheerleading squad? Check. That time Fortune Weathers had perched flirtatiously on his desk, just to copy off his trigonometry quiz? That too. Because here he was with Amelie Adams, a gift from the math-genius gods, and she was . . .

Amazing.

He wasn't starstruck. Jake's mom had plenty of high-profile clients. That chick from *Transformers* had even been at his bar mitzvah. Amelie was different. Totally down-to-earth, funny, and sweet, all in one super-hot package. A package that didn't treat him like he was as undesirable as an outdated Texas Instruments graphing calculator.

Today Amelie wore beat-up jeans that hit the top of her slim hips and a fitted old-school American Apparel baseball shirt, white in the center, with royal blue sleeves and neck. Her red hair was pulled up in a ponytail, her flawless face makeup-free. Her skin was creamy against the flush of her cheeks and the pink of her lips.

Amelie rapped her pencil against the tabletop. "Yoohoo, Jake?"

Her knee brushed his, and Jake drew a sharp breath to stop himself from saying, *I love you*. He felt his heart thudding beneath his burgundy Abercrombie polo shirt.

"Huh? Sorry, long day," Jake smiled sheepishly. "What were you saying?"

"You hungry? I was going to call for some takeout, if that's cool."

Jacob nodded. He hadn't realized until now that he was starving. He hadn't eaten since lunch, and his mom's meager attempt at pastrami on rye was not nearly as filling as the Canter's version she tried to imitate. "Definitely. I know a place that has great carne asada tacos." The words were out of his mouth before he could stop them.

"Oh my God," Amelie said, her shell pink lips forming an O of surprise. "You totally Googled me."

Jake stared at a word problem in his textbook, feeling like a creepy perv. What kind of freak Internet-stalked his tutee? He could practically hear his chances with Amelie drop with a thud to the floor.

"I did," he confessed. "I'm—it wasn't like a creepy thing or something like that. I just . . ."

Amelie play-slapped him on the wrist. "I'm teasing. It's so cute that you did that."

Jacob felt instantly recharged, like someone had put a fresh set of batteries in him. For the first time in his life, a girl was calling him cute. And the girl was *Amelie Adams*.

"Oh, well, yeah, I have my moments." He fought the corners of his mouth as they tried to form a goofy grin. "So, Mexican, then?"

Amelie got up, padding over to a table next to an over-stuffed armchair. She lifted the top of the table and pulled out a pile of menus. "Actually, I'm thinking Greek." She tossed him a menu from Mediterranean Delight. "And then we can watch Meryl Streep movies and maybe have a Harry Potter reading."

Jake laughed, relieved. "Actually, if you like Harry Potter, I bet you'd like the *Golden Compass* books," he said, hoping she wouldn't think his recommendation was lame.

Amelie grabbed his arm excitedly. "I love that series! When I was younger I carried my stuffed teddy bear around, pretending it was my own personal daemon. I was so sad that I was too old to play Lyra when they finally got around to making the movie." She sat back down across from Jake, her blue eyes animated and bright. "Have you read *Automated Alice*?"

Jake shook his head. "No, what's it about?"

"It's this retelling of *Alice in Wonderland* that sort of has a sci-fi twist," Amelie said, getting up to put the stack of menus back. "I think you'd like it."

"You read sci-fi books?" Jake said, eyeing Amelie skeptically.

Amelie shrugged. "A good book is a good book, I don't discriminate. I'm going to bring it for you to borrow next time we have a stalker appointment."

Jacob laughed at her teasing. Was talking to girls always this easy, and he just hadn't known? Or was Amelie just different? It had to be the latter, he decided. She read cool books, and didn't just talk about clothes and boys all the time. He casually flipped open the menu, scanning the list of dinner specials for something without onions—he didn't want to have swamp breath. Not that he'd be trying to kiss Amelie tonight. But maybe soon?

"So, I was thinking," Jacob began, feeling emboldened. "Maybe we should meet up at Urth Caffé on Thursday."

Amelie raised her eyebrows, considering. The last time she'd gone to Urth Caffé she'd been fifteen, and she'd gone with her mom and a William Morris agent eager to poach her from CAA. But Jake wasn't chasing a profitable contract. He just wanted to hang out. Okay, maybe he just wanted to study. But she'd take it. At least when everyone on set left for that evening's hot spot, she could honestly say she had plans with a friend.

"That would be great," she finally said. "Around eight?"

Jake suppressed the urge to jump up and tap the roof of the trailer, like a basketball player who'd just sunk a three-pointer. He hadn't planned to ask Amelie out today, but he'd just done it. And she'd actually said *yes*. He couldn't believe that just last week, he'd thought tutoring meant he'd never have a girlfriend.

Now, it seemed, the bane of his existence had become the key to his happiness.

MISS TACKY TEEN USA

Few things in her short life had really impressed Myla Everhart, but the pool at the Beverly Hills Hotel was one of them. Lined with palm trees and privacy-providing tropical plants, and surrounded by the hotel's trademark green-and-white striped sun chairs, the pool was like Camelot for the celebrity set. A row of cabanas gleamed white as the sun crept toward the west. The sky was a crisp blue, striped with orange and violet clouds. (Fine, so Myla had learned in earth sciences today that they were chemical trails from planes landing at LAX. But why spoil it?)

She rummaged through her bag, clutching the champagne cork invite buried at the bottom. A few art students had created counterfeit versions of the invitation, and it irritated her that non-invitees would probably get into the party. At least she'd stopped Jojo from crashing.

Myla took a deep breath, collecting herself. She was about to enter her first BHH party as a single woman. The last two years, she'd gone to the Splash Bash with Ash, and they'd always ended the evening in one of the hotel's private cabanas. Stupid Ash. He was probably sitting in his room, listening to some whiny L.A. emo band and wishing he hadn't blown it with her.

Pulling down her oversize white Tom Ford sunglasses and smoothing the wrinkles from her floaty cover-up, Myla scanned the pool, already crammed with bodies in various stages of undress. Her eyes narrowed when she saw Billie talking to Ash's friend Tucker. What was *he* doing here?

Before she could stomp over to demand an answer, Ash himself emerged from one of the cabanas in a haze of smoke with Geoff, laughing stupidly. Ash was even wearing the Vilebrequin jellyfish-print trunks she'd given him last summer, as if he still had a right to wear anything Myla had given him.

Myla reached up for her Green Lantern necklace before remembering she'd removed it before school that morning. How dare he show his face here? For the last three years, Myla and her girlfriends had practically been the party's steering committee, planning everything from the guest list to the menu to the dress code. Yes, Ash and his friends had been invited when the corks were distributed in July. But they'd clearly parted ways. They'd split their whole social circle into semicircles, never to be joined again. And he still thought he was welcome at a party that she and her friends had spent hours of time and energy to plan?

Straightening the neckline of her floral print cover-up—in shades of pink and green, to coordinate with her surroundings—Myla tossed her sunglasses into her tote. Her eyes never leaving Ash, she swooped down on him and Geoff.

The guys looked up at her and burst out laughing for no apparent reason, their mouths full of Polo Lounge crab cakes. Clearly, they'd just smoked up. Myla's body tensed with anger. When she and Ash were together, he rarely got high—it made him act like a complete buffoon, and he knew she hated it.

A chunk of half-chewed crab flew from Geoff's mouth and landed within a millimeter of her lime green Dior peep-toe pumps. Kicking the foul food away, she grabbed Ash by the arm and yanked him to a corner of the party.

"What are you doing here? Besides acting like a stoned Neanderthal?"

Ash glared at her angrily, seemingly shaken out of his pot-smoking stupor. "I could ask you the same question."

Myla shook her head. "No, you couldn't." She stared at him violently, her heart palpitating with fury. "You know this is my party. In fact, I should make you and Geoff pay me for the crab cakes, since all the food is on my AmEx. Talia called our catering order months ago. End of discussion. Get out."

Ash crossed his arms over his chest defiantly. His mop of hair was a little damp from a recent dip, and the same troublesome strand as always hung cutely over his left eye. Myla reminded herself that it wasn't her job to push his hair out of his face anymore.

"Yeah, you planned it months ago," Ash retorted. "But my boys and I practically *invented* this party three *years* ago. Remember when the seniors wouldn't let freshmen come to their stupid luau at Hermosa Beach? And

I suggested that we rent the Beverly Hills Hotel pool? If it weren't for me, you'd never have set foot here. You said the hotel was for old people and looked like it was painted with Pepto-Bismol."

Talia and Moira Lacey were drinking daiquiris on sun chairs five feet away, listening to every word. Myla didn't want to make a scene, but she also didn't want to give in to Ash.

"I'm not leaving." She folded her arms across her chest, mimicking Ash's stance.

A waiter stopped next to them with a tray of seared ahi tuna. "Ahi, miss?" She shook her head.

"Thanks," Ash said, grabbing a spear and greedily sucking down the tuna in one fluid motion. "I'm not leaving either," he said, tossing the empty skewer in a garbage can. "And that tuna was good."

"Why do you have to make everything so difficult? We're broken up, and this is my party. Can't you just go hang out in Tucker's garage and pretend you're in some lame band?" Myla narrowed her eyes, waiting for Ash to back down. He always did. Last year, she'd wanted to go to the Rock & Republic show during L.A. Fashion Week, even though Ash had had tickets to see Wolfmother at the Wiltern. In the end, Ash had called the fashion show organizers and had even gotten Myla a spot walking down the runway in R&R's first-ever couture gown.

She didn't get what was up with him the last few days. It was almost like he *didn't* want her back.

Could it be that . . . they were really done?

As the realization overcame her, Myla wouldn't let the tears come. Her jaw formed a hard, angry line. She couldn't believe she'd wasted so many precious hours waiting for Ash to apologize when she could have been accepting their breakup and moving on to the necessary next steps: Get Over It, Get Happy, and her favorite, Get Revenge.

He made a puzzled face. "Hmm, I don't know, Myla. We could try to enjoy ourselves. Create a my-dance-space-your-dance-space situation? Oh, but I forgot—you can't enjoy yourself unless every moment plays out exactly to your specifications."

Myla pulled on her strand of emerald hair angrily. First Jojo had waltzed in and was trying to steal her life. Now Ash was purposely torturing her. Things were not going to her specifications *at all*.

She stormed away and plunked down defiantly in a striped lounge chair next to Talia and Moira.

She was scanning the pool area for a waiter carrying more ahi tuna—*her* favorite—when her eyes landed on Easy Eastman, aka Cassie Eastman, Ash's summer skank. Her melon-y breasts were barely covered by two Day-Glo orange triangles, and half her butt was exposed in an undersize bikini bottom, like she was vying for the title of Miss Tacky Teen USA in her Versace knockoff. She shouldn't have even been at this party, yet she was tottering on four-inch heels next to the pool, sipping from a cosmo and licking her fingers as she put away a miniature Kobe beef burger. A contingent of the boys' water polo team stopped their game of chicken to study Cassie's bikini line while their swim team girlfriends looked on jealously.

"Cassie," Myla called out commandingly.

Cassie looked up, her mouth full. "Myla?" She said it like a question, even though she knew who Myla was. She jiggled over in her heeled mules, a confused look on her face.

"Hi," Myla purred, leaning back in her chair as she scanned Cassie from head to toe. Myla rarely spoke to Easy Eastman. "I love your swimsuit. You just have so much to show off, don't you?"

Cassie nodded vigorously.

"So, I hear you and Ash might get something going."

Fear came over Cassie's face and she looked everywhere but at Myla—at couples feeding each other stuffed mushrooms on lounge chairs, at a cabana filled with fresh-from-the-pool boys resuming a high-stakes poker game, at a group of cheerleaders shrieking as the DJ played their request, that cheesy "Summer Lovin'" song from *Grease.* "Well, um, but—"

"Oh, don't worry about it. I'm so done with him," Myla cooed, grabbing her own cosmo from a passing tray. "It's just, well, you should be ready to invest in some Depends. Ash is great, but he has some unfortunate, ahem, leakage issues. But it's really only a problem if you care about your sheets."

Cassie twirled a lock of her fine blond hair around her finger, looking like the before ad for Fekkai texturizing cream. "So he . . . wets the bed?"

Myla patted Cassie's fake-baked arm. "I didn't want to be vulgar, but . . . yes. But don't worry. That's what adult diapers are for."

Cassie's brow furrowed in concern, as though she'd put all her money on a horse and it had been taken out of the race. Setting down her empty cosmo glass on a low round table, she eyed Myla pleadingly. "So it's probably not worth, you know, pursuing him?"

Myla shook her head. "Oh, no, I don't want to do that to Ash. I mean, he's the kind of guy who really needs a girl-friend. He needs someone patient, you know, a little hand-holding. Because he also has no muscle memory when it comes to kissing. But it's fun, like training a dog. You're just the girl for the job, I bet." Myla glanced around the pool, listening as the gossip traveled in whispers and mur-murs from partiers sprawled in sun loungers to the guys on inflatable rafts drinking Sol. Girls who used to give Ash the eye looked crestfallen as they huddled near a cabana, sipping mai tais and mourning the loss of a crushworthy guy. Yes, bed wetting was cliché, but it worked.

Myla stood and patted one of Cassie's arms in a dis-play of faux sisterhood. She clipped past Cassie on her towering shoes. Her work here was done.

Ash leaned back in his sun chair, the flaps of his white cabana opened wide so he could watch cute girls walk by as he, Tucker, and Geoff chowed down on the hotel's oversize sirloin burgers. In Ash's estimation, it was the first time he'd ever gotten the last word in with Myla, and he'd ordered a big meal to celebrate.

Mark Bauman popped his head in the tent, his artfully windswept man-bangs practically glued to his forehead. "Dude, are you okay?"

Ash took a swig of his Stella, wiping his mouth with the back of his hand. "Course. Got my burger, got a brew, chicks walking by. It's a good day."

Mark bit his thumbnail, which made him look even girlier than usual. "Uh, well, people are saying shit."

"Yeah, like what?" Geoff asked, the ground beef in his mouth on display.

Tucker sat up, his pale blue eyes flashing eagerly. "Stuff about the new girl? Is Myla's sister here? And, dudes, I don't believe any of the rumors about her. Except maybe that she's a sex addict." He squeezed his eyes shut, crossing his fingers as though wishing for her. "Lailah 2.0, Lailah 2.0," he chanted goofily.

Ash wondered if she was here, or if Myla had excluded her from the guest list. He wouldn't put it past her to make life extra-difficult for a new sibling, just for fun. Of course, why would Jojo even want to come to the party, with all the shit being said about her? One of today's top "fun facts" was that Jojo didn't come from Sacramento but had escaped from some religious cult in Montana.

Mark grimly shook his head. "No, they're saying . . . that Ash, like, slobbers everywhere when he kisses a girl. Plus . . ." Mark mumbled the last words, and Ash could barely hear him.

"Dude, what was the last thing?" Tucker leaned forward, rubbing the blond fuzz near his tanned temple.

"Thathemightpissthebed," Mark blurted, clutching his forehead anxiously, panic in his eyes. Last year, he'd been hanging out with the Young Environmentalist Club as he tried to gain entry into Ash's crowd. Now that he'd finally made it to the big leagues, he looked nervous at being the bearer of bad news.

The applewood bacon Ash had been savoring moments

earlier started to taste sour. This was definitely Myla's work.

A muscled arm shoved Mark out of Ash's line of view. Then, a face he hated appeared in the open cabana.

Lewis Buford.

Lewis's haughty, handsome face wore a shit-eating grin. He wore a Boss collared shirt open to the chest over a pair of fitted Diesel swim trunks. Behind him stood two members of his entourage—Aaron Davies, a creepy thirty-five-year-old nightclub promoter who hit on high school chicks, and Barnsley Toole, a Hollywood wannabe who clung to whoever could get him in *Us Weekly*.

"Gilmour, it's nice to hear you and Myla finally split," Lewis said, his tanned face twisted into a half smirk, half pervy leer beneath his dark, slicked-back hair. Ash's hands formed involuntary fists. Why did Lewis have to catch him off guard like this? Sitting in this stupid tent, half-naked, was not Ash's ideal scenario in which to go mano a mano with this jerkbag.

Myla had introduced Ash and Lewis back in freshman year, after Ash had said he wanted to start a band. So Ash and Lewis had formed the Storms, and they hatched all kinds of plans for their cosmic rise to stardom. They even cowrote one song, "Deadly Kiss." But then Lewis told Ash he was sick of playing bass and wanted to be lead singer, even though Ash had the better voice. When Ash wouldn't give in, Lewis threw a fit—even kicking in the face of the vintage Fender Ash had bought on eBay. Since then, Lewis had formed several unenduring bands on his own, and had tried to cozy up to Myla on more than one occasion, usually when she and Ash were fighting. Now, Lewis thought he was hot shit because he hung out with all of hipster Hollywood, checking out bands at the Troubador and the Roxy trying to find rising stars for his upstart record label, Deadly Kiss—he wasn't even creative enough to come up with a new name.

"Go fuck yourself, Buford," Ash spat, standing up from the low chair and stepping closer to Lewis. Lewis didn't flinch. A crowd at the bar was watching, drinking up the exchange like a chaser for their tequila shots.

"Hey man, don't get all touchy just because you've got leaky equipment." Lewis raised one eyebrow.

"Dude, why don't you go find a band to screw up?" It was the best Ash could come up with. He pushed his way out of the cabana into the sun, Lewis's shadow falling over him.

"Don't change the subject, Gilmour," Lewis sneered, as though they were in a sarcasm showdown at the OK Corral. "Why don't you take a swim? Or can your huggies not get wet?" Barnsley threw back his head, his preppy yellow-blond hair immobile as he giggled like a hyena.

Ash shoved past Lewis and dove into the pool, toppling a couple making out on an oversize inner tube. He swam across, climbed out quickly, and yanked a towel off a beach chair. Dripping wet, he stomped barefoot through the Polo Lounge and into the hotel lobby. He shivered, not from cold but rage. Lewis was the shit-covered cherry on top of Myla's poison-laced sundae. She was acting like this whole big battle between them had been his idea, when *she* was the one who'd walked out on *him*. And not just that day at his house: She'd walked out on him for the whole summer—and hadn't even felt bad about it.

Yeah, in the past when they'd fought, he'd given in, but this was so much bigger than an argument about whether to hang out with her girlfriends at the Beverly Center or his buds at the beach. It hit Ash like one of those ocean waves that start calm and then slap you in the gut: They really were over. Myla wasn't going to appeal to him for mercy. He swallowed hard, fighting his burger, his beer, and the tuna as they tried to make the return trip up his throat.

The lobby was like a ghost town, most of the hotel's fabulous guests having already stepped out for late-night dinner reservations or club hopping. Ash trailed chlorine-scented water onto the pink and green carpet. Only one chair was occupied, the girl in it sitting with her back to him. Her shiny almond-colored hair was pulled into a low ponytail at the nape of her neck. She turned at the sound of Ash's soggy footfalls. He recognized her instantly— Myla's new sister. In the throes of his newfound crush, Tucker had cut Jojo's picture from a copy of *Us Weekly* and tacked it up in his locker under the words, "Hottie alert."

She was cute. Beautiful, actually, but not in the same check-me-out way as Myla. She had Lailah's pronounced cheekbones and captivating eyes, with Barkley's open, easy, down-to-earth expression.

She looked surprised as Ash approached her. "Hey, you're Jojo, Myla's sister, right? What are you doing out here?" He stood in front of her, drops of water falling from his hair onto Jojo's forehead.

Jojo wiped away the water trickling into her eyes. Ash Gilmour was cuter up close than from afar at BHH.

He was Myla's ex-boyfriend, she knew, because that gossip was so big that even a loser like her heard murmurs of it.

He had sandy blond hair, slightly uneven on the bottom, with a piece falling in front of his warm brown eyes, which had tiny flecks of amber in them. Jojo suppressed a smile at his beyond-dorky, jellyfish-adorned swim trunks.

"I wasn't invited," she said simply, her fingers playing with the glossy corners of September's *Vogue*.

How predictable, Ash thought. Myla was playing Screw with the New Girl. She'd done the same thing when Billie Bollman—now one of her closest friends—was new to their school in eighth grade. Myla, intimidated by Billie's long blond hair and even longer legs, had started a rumor that Billie left her school in Malibu because she'd had an affair with a lesbian badminton coach. Ash bet she was threatened by having a new sister, especially one who could compete in the looks category—not to mention being her parents' biological progeny.

Ash settled himself, still wet, into the chair next to Jojo's, pulling it close. "You're not missing much," he said, rubbing his hair dry with a fluffy green towel. A white-haired man and woman in matching plaid golf outfits entered through the glass double doors, sniffing disapprovingly at the sight of a barefoot, shirtless, and soaked teenager tilting back so comfortably in his chair. "Unless I'm mistaken and you're actually a fan of Myla."

Jojo smiled wanly. "We're not exactly close."

Maybe it was the shock of the cold water in the air-conditioned lobby, but suddenly Ash felt charged. "You know, we could have a little fun," he said, casually tap-ping the arm of the chair. "Myla doesn't seem to love you, and she definitely hates me."

Jojo turned her violet eyes on him in a questioning, "where are you going with this?" stare.

Ash licked his lips excitedly. "Well, think about it. If you and I pretend to be friends, Myla will go nuts."

For the first time since Ash had sat down, Jojo's smile reached her eyes. No, it went past her eyes—it lifted her entire body. It was a little manipulative, maybe even cruel . . . but wasn't that the Myla Everhart way?

"You know, Ash, I like the way you think."

BELIEVE THE HYPE

"Come on, powder puff, in what universe does a girl like me go out with a jock like Tommy?"

Kady and Amelie were sitting across from each other at the tiny IKEA table in Amelie's trailer on Thursday afternoon, scripts laid out in front of them.

Kady had come asking for Amelie's help because Gary, the nervous new director—the producers had fired Dirk Wink and hired Gary, the AD—had pulled her aside to say he expected her to nail her scenes tomorrow. They'd done fourteen takes of Kady and DeAndra's confrontational, alpha-versus-beta scene, and Gary still wasn't satisfied, so they were reshooting the whole thing.

Amelie had been grateful for the unexpected company, even if it was Kady's first offer to hang out in days. She could use the distraction. She'd spent the last hour on the couch with today's *Hollywood Reporter,* staring at Hunter's head shot. He'd been signed for a part in the next *Iron Man* movie, as the hero's illegitimate son, and had been busy dealing with contract negotiations. He'd hardly been on set, and even when he had, he and Amelie had barely spoken. She was starting to feel like Class Angel all the time: completely invisible.

"True love *should* be surprising, Lizzie."

Amelie knew she wasn't exactly putting her heart into Class Angel's pep talk. Here she was, doling out sage advice about true love when she couldn't even get her true love to talk to her.

"But me with Tommy is almost sacrilege," Kady over-emoted, throwing her hands up as she read it. "I'll never have any street cred in the art world wearing a letterman's jacket."

Kady flipped the pages closed. "Forget it." She sighed. "I'm as good as I'm going to be." She pushed her red plastic chair away from the table and padded into the trailer's tiny bedroom.

"Your trailer's nicer than mine," Kady said, her throaty tomboy voice echoing in the smallish space. "It pays to be Fairy Princess, huh?" Kady examined a pair of tiger lily orange Austrian crystal chandelier earrings. All of the pristine white *Class Angel* outfits were strewn across the generic-looking beige bedspread. Kady had also unearthed a selection of sparkly tops the wardrobe people had assembled for Amelie to wear during cast interviews for the DVD extras.

"Not that I mind, but what are you doing?" Amelie asked. She leaned against the doorjamb, genuinely curious.

"Picking out an outfit for your clubbing debut, happening—dun dah dah—tonight!" Kady swung a nearly sheer black Chelsea Flower embroidered top with a low-cut neckline in front of Amelie's face.

Seeing Amelie's grimace, Kady held the top up in front of her. "Don't argue, you're coming out with us tonight. You can say no Friday, Saturday, and Sunday, but I'm insisting on Thursday. It's the best night of the week. And you don't have to be here tomorrow. Just DeAndra and I, doing that same scene over and over until we die." It was true—Amelie didn't have to report to the set tomorrow. Kady and DeAndra did, however, as did fifty members of the crew who'd been supposed to have the day off, to finally get their scene to Gary's liking.

Amelie turned to face her mirror. The top had been rejected for a DVD interview because it was too sexy. She tossed it back on the bed. "Look, I appreciate you inviting me, but I have tuto—I'm meeting a friend tonight, at Urth Caffé. And some Kidz Net promos to shoot tomorrow morning. And, I just . . . can't. It's a big deal I'm even doing a PG movie. It's a lot for my fans to get used to. If I start partying—"

Kady's pressed an emerald green D&G halter with practically no back to Amelie's frame. "You'll what? Be doing something for Amelie Adams, instead of Fairy Princess?"

Amelie took the green top and threw it back down with the rest. "It's just not my thing." The words sounded hollow, even to her. She *did* want to go. But if Lindsay Lohan or Britney Spears had grown up with the Board looming over them, maybe things would have turned out differently for them.

Kady sighed and flopped her petite frame onto the bed, wrinkling several thousand dollars in designer apparel as she did so. "I didn't want to play this card, but I will."

She paused dramatically and folded her arms cockily over her requisite black Lizzie Barnett T-shirt. "Hunter will be there," she said slyly, one eyebrow raised, a knowing twinkle in her blue eyes.

Amelie silently studied the individual links of a silver lariat necklace on the oak vanity table. She couldn't bring herself to look at Kady.

"I saw you talking the other day. You're in Puppy-Love City." Kady sprang up again, rifling through the piles of clothing.

Amelie blushed. She thought she'd been so discreet. "But I thought you and Hunter were—"

"Puh-lease! Hunter's so not my style. I like 'em skinny, scraggly, and a little punk rock." Kady threw her head back and laughed, her Chiclet-white teeth visible in her dainty mouth. "Ew. I sound like a total ho."

Kady contemplated her ho-ness for a second before throwing herself against a down pillow. "You know you want to goooo," she singsonged.

Amelie toyed with the sequins on a black ABS mini-dress. She was relieved that there was nothing between Kady and Hunter, but that didn't change her situation. "What will I tell my mom? She's expecting me at home tonight."

Kady gave her a playful "Duh!" shove. "Have you never *seen* a teen comedy? You're sleeping over at my house. Actually, we'll head there now to get ready before we hit Area. I think your sweet face could use some black eyeliner."

Amelie stood up from the bed, taking the sequined dress with her. She held it in front of her and looked in the mirror. Its scooped neckline was tasteful, but the skirt was dangerously short.

Amelie pictured herself standing at the edge of the dance floor, looking grown-up and enticing. Sexy. Hunter would ask her to dance. Did people get asked to dance at clubs? She wasn't sure. But she knew she had no chance with Hunter if she didn't play the game a little.

She picked her cell phone up off the nightstand, dialing her mom. "Hi Mom, it's me. I'm fine. I just wanted to let you know I'm going to spend the night at Kady's house. She rented the new Natalie Portman movie and I haven't seen it yet," she lied, both loving and hating how easy this was. Kady gave her the thumbs-up. "I will. Love you, too."

She hung up, her body jittering like she'd pounded a five-shot venti soy latte. She couldn't wait to get to Area so Hunter could see her in the black dress. She wouldn't wear a trace of Fairy Princess pink or Class Angel white.

Tonight, she was playing the part of Amelie Adams, a young starlet ready to have some fun.

SUPERBAD NIGHT

Myla swung open the door to her house, dodging a wayward Nerf dart headed straight for her eye. The dart hit Lailah's Oscar, nested cozily on the teak table her father had made himself. Myla had heard the electric saw running in the wood shop yesterday, her dad busily building Jojo her "permanent vacation" furniture, an enormous armoire. Myla briefly wondered if once completed, it would be big enough to lock her new sister inside.

"Got you!" Nelson shrieked, appearing from behind a potted palm to retrieve his dart. He bounded over to Myla and wrapped her knees in a paralytic grip—or a hug, depending on how you looked at it. He looked up at her, his long curls forming a messy halo, "Hi, My-My. You mine."

Myla softened at the nickname, loosening Nelson's death grip so she didn't go flying head over Dolce & Gabbana white patent pumps. She kissed his forehead. Secretly, Myla really liked all the babies. It was her newest sibling that got on her nerves. Maybe being extra sweet to her other siblings could score her enough good karma to make Jojo go away.

Not that Jojo had been in her face, or anything. After the pool party, Myla had expected to find Jojo in a pouty state, eager to tattle on Myla to Mom and Dad. But Jojo had been serene, waiting comfortably in the lobby, a Mona Lisa smile on her face and the September *Vogue* open on her lap. Maybe she'd finally figured out that being seen and not heard—at least by Myla—was still better than Crap-ramento. And there'd been no whiny text messages from Ash, which was just fine. She had nothing to say to him anyway. Since he'd made his big swan-dive exit from the pool party, she hadn't seen him once at school.

Myla cut through the dining room, her heels leaving little circular imprints on the handwoven rug her parents had purchased at a street market in Cairo this summer. The nanny, a chubby English girl who designed handbags in her downtime, was helping eight-year-old Mahalo read *Willie Wonka and the Chocolate Factory* as Barkley looked on, providing a nasally voice for the Willie Wonka lines. Briefly she wondered where Jojo was. She'd missed their three o'clock pickup today, sending a curt text message at three fifteen: You can leave without me. I've made other arrangements. Had Jojo ever made it home? Myla quickly dismissed the thought. She didn't have time to worry about Jojo's whereabouts. She was probably hanging with her new loser friend, Jacob Porter-Goldsmith.

Myla waved in her dad's direction, anxious to get to her room and pop on a DVD. She, Talia, and Billie had hit the Beverly Center right after school, and Myla's feet and legs ached from lugging around her purchases. So far, the Myla-and-Ash split had been going okay. Tosha Saunders and Mai Halen, two super-obnoxious cheerleaders who thought their red-and-white polyester BHH uniforms were just as fashion-forward as Missoni sweaterdresses, had been hanging around Myla's crew, thinking they were part of the group. But after respective makeout sessions with Ash's friends Geoff and Tucker at the pool party, they'd finally defected to Ash's side. Meanwhile, Julius Grand and Simon Todd had made their way to Myla's group because Julius was into the Lacey twins—he'd take either one, or better yet, both—and Simon did whatever Julius said. Everything had ended up just as Myla had outlined it in her Moleskine.

Now that her most loyal followers had made themselves known, Myla needed to do something nice to prove they'd chosen the right side. Maybe a little chartered-jet jaunt to the Palms in Vegas, or a laid-back off-season weekend at her parents' mountain cabin in Big Bear.

Flinging open the door to her room, Myla was vaguely annoyed to find that David, her driver, hadn't yet brought up her shopping bags. She closed and locked her door behind her. She didn't need him barging in here when she was lounging in her jammies.

She'd cleared as much Ash memorabilia as she could from her room—all the framed photos she used to keep on her huge vanity were now in a box from her latest Charles David purchase—but she still saw signs of him everywhere. Atop her white cube-shaped twelve-drawer dresser—printed with Andy Warhol's daisies in different hues—where a cigar box filled with ticket stubs from every concert and movie she and Ash had been to in the last three years sat. On her king-size Charles Rogers plank bed, a stuffed SpongeBob Ash had won her at some cheesy Venice Beach carnival stared at her blankly. At least her closet—custom-size so that skirts, pants, tops, dresses, and jeans each got twelve feet of hanger space— was void of Ash Gilmour memorabilia. She'd always told him to never buy her clothing. Scanning her space, she took minor satisfaction in knowing that Jojo's room next door was at least 250 square feet smaller.

Myla opened her built-in DVD cabinet, scanning the titles and settling on *Superbad*. The raunchy comedy would perfectly suit her victorious mood, and secretly she found Michael Cera cute. Popping the DVD in, she freed her feet from their treacherous shoes and flopped down on her purple velvet couch, running her bare toes over her sheepskin rug. She skipped ahead to the scene where Michael Cera ran from the cops. As his character, Evan, zoomed down the street on her fifty-two-inch flat screen, Myla heard muffled peals of laughter coming from next door. Jojo's room. The unmistakable Mario Kart music made it impossible to concentrate on Seth Rogen puffing out, "Fastest kid in the world." Myla rolled her eyes. Jojo was probably playing online against some loser in Sacramento.

Myla stomped out of her room and banged on Jojo's door. "Do you mind? I'm trying to watch a movie." She turned the knob and burst inside.

Jojo was sprawled on her own burgundy velvet couch. And sitting beside her, his hair mussed and his eyes glimmering, was Ash.

What the fuck? What. The. Fuck.

Jojo hit pause on her Wii steering wheel and the game

froze on Mario throwing a turtle shell. Ash blandly waved in her direction, like he wanted to get back to his game.

Myla eyed her "sister." She wore a cream Michael Stars racerback tank, paired with ivory Hudson jeans that had been sold out when Myla hit Kitson last week. Three gold leather bangles adorned her tanned wrist and a gold Dior heart pendant hung daintily around her neck. On her feet were garden-variety Havaianas flip-flops in white, each with a tiny golden daisy affixed to the outside strap. Her hair was fastened in a stylishly messy updo with plain old Chinese restaurant chopsticks, several strands falling loosely around her face. She practically glowed—her face was flushed in a way not even professionally applied Tarte cheek stain could mimic.

"Where did you get those jeans?" Myla fired off, her lips set in a sneer.

Jojo looked down, as though she'd forgotten what she was wearing. "Oh, these?" she asked lightly. "Mom and I went shopping. She thought they'd look good on me."

Myla breathed out through her clenched teeth, closing her eyes tightly and hoping that when she opened them Jojo would be gone, Ash would be waiting for her in her room, and *she'd* be wearing the ivory jeans. She opened her eyes. Jojo was smiling at her as though playing Wii in her room with Ash Gilmour were the most natural thing in the world.

"Did you want to play?" she asked sweetly, holding out the steering wheel.

Myla absently shook her head, processing the direness of the last four days. First, she and Ash had mutated from three-year golden couple to spiteful exes. Then her parents' bio-kid had shown up like some perky nightmare. Now, the two forces that had utterly fucked up her life were laughing together over a Wii game. Myla was not equipped to handle this kind of mindfuck. Did Ash like her sister now? Had her parents decided their real kid was better than her?

Myla marched back into her bedroom and grabbed the Rolling Stones T-shirt from its place on her desk. She'd left it there so it wouldn't mix with her other clothes and erase Ash's scent. Next to her laptop, she spotted a scissors. Impulsively, she snatched them up. Not even bothering to look in the mirror, she snipped the green strand out of her hair.

Rolling the tendril of hair in the soft cotton of the shirt, Myla flew back to Jojo's room, where Ash and Jojo had resumed their game. She flung the balled-up shirt at Ash, hitting him squarely in the face. His kart careened wildly off the track as locks of Myla's hair fell onto the arm of the couch.

"I don't need this anymore," she hissed, turning on her bare heels and vanishing as a confused Ash pulled the shirt away from his face.

She slammed her door and cranked up *Superbad* to full volume. She needed a good laugh tonight.

Jojo didn't think it was possible, but Myla Everhart's lower lip had trembled. Actually trembled. She smiled slightly, barely paying attention as Ash knocked his kart into hers, sending her Baby Mario flying off a cliff. He bumped his shoulder into hers as his Donkey Kong drifted around a curve, shooting smoke from the kart's tailpipe.

"Aw, poor Baby Mario fall off a cliff?" he teased in a baby-talk voice.

Jojo laughed. "Why don't you pick on someone your own size?" A cloud character dropped Baby Mario back onto the track and Jojo accelerated, only to send her kart flying back off the cliff she'd just returned from.

Ash shook his head, grinning, as he shoulder-nudged her again.

For the first time since she'd landed at Burbank Airport, Jojo didn't feel like some random cousin from the boonies who was staying at Barbar's house. Lailah had taken her shopping up and down Robertson Boulevard after school today, telling Jojo she'd look "beautiful" in whatever she picked out. It was different shopping with a mom than it had been with her dads, who always looked uneasy hanging out outside the dressing room as Jojo tried things on. Jojo had been so mesmerized by the amazing boutiques on Robertson that she'd missed her dads' call from the tundra. She felt bad, since she didn't want to call them back after she and Lailah got home—it was almost 4 a.m. in Greenland.

Not only had her plan worked, but Ash was totally fun to have around. He'd brought over carryout sushi from Katsuya and his Wii, and it didn't seem to matter to either of them if Myla even discovered them hanging out tonight. Of course, the fact that she had gave Jojo a rush like she'd just scored the game-winning goal.

They wrapped up their race, Ash finishing in fifth and Jojo last, probably from driving on autopilot. Ash turned to her, his eyes filled with energy. He held up his hand for a high-five, and Jojo obliged.

"Nice work. I mean, not in that race, because that was
the worst driving I've ever seen. Remind me never to let
you drive in Laurel Canyon." Ash tossed his steering wheel
on the cushion next to him, his dark brown eyes laughing.
"But before. We really pissed her off. Although . . . there's
green hair all over your couch."

Jojo shrugged. "Whatever. Maybe she'll try to be a little nicer now. I'd feel bad if she kept cutting off her hair.
Though maybe then people would think *she* has head
lice." Jojo smirked.

Ash laughed, and Jojo felt warmth spread through her
chest.

"By the way," she added, raising a teasing eyebrow,
"way to steal my gossip thunder. I thought I had it
locked with Mormon cults and meth addictions, but then
you sweep on in and make it the Ash show." That Jake
guy had totally called it. She'd have to tell him when she
bumped into him again.

Ash cleared his throat and stared at her very seriously.
"Yeah, I can't believe you even let me sit on your couch.
You better watch out—next I might get in your bed."

Jojo blushed. She looked away, unable to meet his
eyes.

"Holy shit, that sounded dirty." Ash threw his shaggy
blond head against the cushion and laughed.

Jojo giggled too, admiring the way Ash's eyes crinkled
when he smiled. He didn't even seem to care that the
whole school was talking about him and saying things
that weren't true. How could he be so cool about everything?

He patted Jojo's arm, leaving his hand resting near her

elbow. "Don't worry, though. Myla deserves this. She's so used to getting her way all the time." Ash shifted on the couch so that he faced Jojo. "She pretty much has all of our high school on red alert, wrapped around her little finger, you know?'

Jojo plucked a few long, silken strands of green hair off Ash's shoulder. "Well, it makes sense."

Ash nodded. "Yeah, she can be pretty scary."

Jojo slapped his arm. "No, I mean, *look* at her. It's ridiculous how pretty she is. Even surrounded by other pretty people, she's still the Queen of Hotness." She pursed her lips. "Sometimes, I wonder if I'm *lucky* she doesn't like me. If we were friends, I'd always be comparing myself to her," she said honestly. She'd never felt competitive around Willa, the way she did around Myla. As much as she resented Myla's bitchiness, in truth, she was just intimidated. And a little jealous.

Ash leaned back again, turning his head so that he was looking up at Jojo. "Yeah, she's gorgeous, I'm not going to argue with that. But don't sell yourself short."

"You don't have to lie." Jojo felt herself blush. "I'm cool with it. Some people are just average—they won't make you vomit, but they won't make you faint, either. They're Sacramento. And some people have so much perfection in one package that it makes sense for the world to revolve around them. They're L.A. It's just how it is." She shrugged. After five days here, judging everything L.A. against its Sacramento equivalent, she'd decided it was no use even to compare them—they were worlds apart.

"Did you actually get knocked in the head with one

of those turtle shells?" Ash shot back. He scooted closer to Jojo on the couch, playfully pulling one of the chopsticks from her hair, watching it tumble to her shoulders. "Look, you're as cool as any girl at BHH, maybe cooler, since you beat me at Wii bowling. And you're definitely L.A. Not Sacramento. You're pretty. Beautiful. Et cetera. Try chanting it in the mirror once in a while. It works for Myla."

Ash's tone was serious as he locked eyes with Jojo. Jojo didn't look away. She felt like she was swimming in his amazing brown-eyed gaze.

As he flipped the chopstick around in his hand, Jojo caught a glimpse of her reflection in the now-blank television screen. In her lips and eyes, she saw a trace of her mind-blowingly beautiful mother. And she *was* good at Wii bowling.

The heat in Jojo's chest expanded and spread throughout her body. Ash Gilmour was her sister's ex, and the cutest guy at Beverly Hills High.

And he liked Jojo Milford.

CUT HIM SOME SLACKS

Jake took another sip of his second Spanish latte. Urth Caffé was crammed with Angelenos looking for a late-day caffeine fix. Young mothers fresh out of evening yoga classes queued together, aligned like disciples behind an alpha mom who bragged about the unstructured play camp her kids had attended over the summer. A couple near Jake was having a vicious fight in fakely melodic tones. "I hate your face," the petite brunette girlfriend said, though her inflection said, I made cookies for you.

Jacob had chosen a table in the corner farthest from the register that overlooked Beverly Boulevard. Amelie Adams still hadn't shown for their—was it a date? An appointment? A meeting? Whatever it was, she was half an hour late. He hadn't really wanted a second latte, but had ordered just so he could keep the table.

Stay cool, he told himself, looking onto Beverly at a trio of Loyola-Marymount girls walking by in oversize LMU sweatshirts and eating cones from Cold Stone Creamery. His Corolla, which he'd washed and waxed right after school, was sandwiched between a Mercedes and a Jaguar, looking as hopeless and awkward as Jake felt.

Jake's phone let out its electronic trill. Agitated by the noise, three miniature poodles wearing matching polka-dot sweaters started yapping, straining against their leashes. The woman holding the leash, her diamond white hair in a short pageboy, shot Jacob a dirty look. She could only muster a half-frown, thanks to brows lifted so much they seemed to float at the lower edge of her forehead.

Jake's phone issued its standard-issue ringtone once more. He'd wanted to pick a song for his ringtone, but had feared picking something lame. He grabbed his cell, a no-frills Motorola with iffy caller ID, off the table before it rang again and permanently destroyed Urth's Zen vibe. The number came up unavailable. Maybe it was Amelie, calling from down the street to explain why she was late. He tried to lower his voice as he answered. "Hello?"

"She there yet?" Miles practically screamed into the phone. Jake could hear the sounds of Halo 3 in the background.

"No, Miles." Jake sighed and hung up. It was Miles's second call in five minutes. Last night, Jake had gone to Miles's house to start working on their honors chemistry project. Jake had bragged about his date with Amelie, and Miles, who poured himself into every project—he'd camped out overnight for tickets to the new *Batman* movie, even though they were available on Fandango— had been determined to help Jake strategize for his date. Neither he nor Jake had ever nabbed a yes from the opposite sex, so Miles had taken up the mantle of Jake's dating coach. He'd even checked out twelve back issues of *Details* from the Beverly Hills Public Library. Thanks to his reading, Miles had already commended Jake on inviting Amelie to Urth Caffé instead of somewhere more generic, like Coffee Bean. He also suggested that Jake scout the area for good places to go afterward, in case the date went well and she wanted to keep hanging out. "You need to put a lot of thought into it in advance, but make the suggestion casually, so that you never seem like you're trying too hard," he'd lectured. Jake was regretting telling Miles about the date in the first place.

Jake's phone rang again. This time, Miles's number showed on the screen. Jake answered. "Stop calling!" he hissed into the phone. The barista, a wiry guy with dreadlocks, scowled at him. Jake had a feeling the guy never gave that kind of dirty look to the CAA agents who frequented this place with their Bluetooths firmly embedded in their skulls.

Jake hung up. She was forty minutes late now. How much longer should he wait?

An hour later, the coffee shop was mostly empty. The dreadlocked barista wiped down the counter with cucumber-scented organic cleaner, the fresh smell mingling with the aroma of ground coffee beans. The romance gods were not smiling on the couple in the corner, either. Their argument was still taking place in singsongy tones that seemed even more menacing now, with no sound system or coffee shop din to absorb them.

"I've never respected your work," chirped the girlfriend, cutely twirling a pigtail around her finger.

"I only liked you for your body," the guy slung back, in a tone reserved for adorable toddlers.

Jake stared at the leaf painted in foam on his latest latte's surface. The douche-y barista had felt bad for him and had given him a drink on the house. Jake had had three coffees, though, and now just wished he could use a restroom. He worried if he did, Amelie would arrive while he was peeing and think he'd left.

What if she'd only looked for him outside? Or thought he told her to meet him at Coffee Bean, a few blocks away? Jake sighed, rubbing his curly hair in agony.

Then the door chimed, and Jake perked up—it sounded just like Fairy Princess's magical wand wave. Amelie was finally here. Jake pretended to be fixing his hair, not hanging his head in sorrow. He looked up at the door, hoping his face didn't betray how excited and eager he was.

Miles stood by the door, wearing his favorite *Not a Cylon* shirt, shaking his head at Jake. He looked around the small café, where there were no spots Amelie could have hidden, except maybe behind a display of free-trade coffee for sale.

"Dude, she's not here," Miles said, pushing his horn-rimmed glasses up his nose. He'd just ordered a new pair of Giorgio Armani hipster frames after seeing them in *Details* on some guy who was dating Natalie Portman.

"I know," Jake said, irritated.

"She in the bathroom?" Miles again craned his neck to look down the hallway, as though he had X-ray vision and could see through the bathroom doors. Miles was the kind of guy who wouldn't even think to use X-ray glasses for pornographic purposes—he'd want them just because they were cool.

Miles scanned Jake from head to toe. "Man, what are you doing?" he said, pulling out a chair to sit. He pointed at Jake's khakis. "My dad wears pants like those to do taxes in." Jake looked down, offended. He'd chosen the Dockers because he thought they made his upper body appear more defined. He'd paired them with Nike running shoes that were a little worn in, and a bright green polo shirt.

"They're just pants," he protested, as Miles laid claim to the untouched latte. He took a sip that left a foam mustache.

"According to *Details*, pants are never just pants, and those are slacks," Miles said, throwing up his hands. "Chicks like Amelie Adams don't date guys who wear slacks."

Jake narrowed his eyes. "She's not here, remember? How would she have seen what I'm wearing?"

Miles shook his head. "Maybe she came, saw you standing there in your Midwestern Dad outfit, and left. What were you wearing when you first met her?"

Jake thought back. "Um, my math camp shirt and jeans. But she thought the shirt was from Fred Segal."

Miles took a deep, contemplative breath, like he was about to tell a ten-year-old there was no Santa Claus. "Jake, this is a disaster. All your jeans are sky blue."

Jake was beyond annoyed. What did sky blue jeans have to do with anything? Amelie had stood him up. Now he wanted to get home before he was locked in the shop overnight. "What color are jeans supposed to be?"

Miles gestured with his head at the still-arguing couple behind him. "Look at that guy," he said. "He's in Rogan distressed denim. Fashion jeans. Notice that they are dark, not light, blue," Miles lectured. "His girlfriend may hate him, but she can't argue that he's got no style."

Jake looked at the guy's jeans. He guessed they did look cool, especially the way the minutely frayed bottoms fell over the guy's shoes, a pair of vintage-looking burgundy Pumas.

"See? You need some new clothes," Miles said, looking like he was composing Jake's before-and-after photo spread for *Details*. "Fred Segal, Kitson, American Rag. How much do you have saved from math camp?"

Jake quickly did a mental calculation. Enough to fill up the Corolla forty times over. Or enough for a wardrobe worthy of Amelie Adams's boyfriend.

The choice was simple.

NIGHT OF THE HUNTER

"Hey, it's Fairy Princess! Can I take my picture with you?" A guy in a white jacket and dark jeans whose breath reeked of Stella Artois threw an arm over Amelie's shoulder. He'd snapped a camera phone photo of the two of them before Amelie even knew what was going on.

Kady leaned back in her wide armchair and giggled at the overwhelmed look on Amelie's face. White, mod-'60s décor was the motif at Area, a nightclub in West Hollywood that was surprisingly still hot even after being open for a few years. On a dance floor the size of a three-car garage, dancers fought for room to demonstrate their sex appeal to the tune of Duffy's "Mercy." Sequins and skin were on equal display beneath a ceiling of recessed lights in rainbow hues.

Kady, Amelie, and their crowd sat in a banquette along the dance floor's outer edge. Similar seating surrounded the dance area, and every booth was packed. Along the outskirts of the club, fatigued dancers leaned back in buttery leather Warhol-era furniture and couples shamelessly made out.

Kady poured herself another flute of Veuve, passing

the bottle to Amelie, who quickly handed it to Moira Lacey. It was 1:30 a.m., and Amelie had passed up alcohol for a few hours now. She wanted to have fun, but that didn't mean she had to get drunk.

"You look bored," Kady commented, as Duffy faded into a new track by the Virgins. "Maybe it's time you had a drink."

Amelie *was* bored. Bored with scanning the crowd every two seconds to see if she noticed traces of Hunter's broad shoulders and dark hair. She'd joined Kady and the other girls on the dance floor several times, shimmying with all the enthusiasm of a marionette controlled by a Xanax-addled puppeteer. Now she just wanted to go home—actually, back to Kady's, given the lie she'd told her mom—crawl into bed, and sleep off the whole experience. She wasn't a nightclub person, plain and simple. Plus, the last time she'd gotten up to dance, she'd remembered that she'd totally blown off her tutoring session with Jake. All because her mind had been filled with Hunter, who wasn't even here. Now the guilt of ditching Jake clung to her like a sticky film.

"I'm fine," Amelie said, smiling weakly. She didn't want to hurt Kady's feelings, or worse, come off as judgmental. "Thanks for bringing me out with you."

DJ Homicide faded the Virgins into "Shut Up and Let Me Go," and DeAndra squealed, "I love this song—let's dance!"

Staring at the area somewhere over Amelie's shoulder, Kady nodded. "Yeah. Amelie, you probably want to wait here."

The other girls got up, bouncing their way to the dance

floor. Amelie felt like a jerk. Had she offended Kady? Sitting alone in the banquette, Amelie turned to catch sight of her group now on the dance floor. Maybe if she joined them, she could patch things up with Kady.

Amelie stood up from the cushy seat, bumping into the shoulder of a guy who had been about to sit down. "Sorry, no more pictures," Amelie said, speaking to the guy's arm.

"Amelie?" Hunter's unmistakably deep voice cut under the poppy beat. Amelie looked up to find herself staring into his dark, liquid eyes. A shiver careened through her, rattling every sequin on her dress. Hunter wore dark jeans and a plain dark blue button-down shirt, open at the collar. His normally stoic face bore traces of surprise.

"Kady told me you might come out tonight," he said, rubbing the back of his neck. "But I'm kind of surprised you actually did. Glad, too."

Amelie hoped her face wasn't shiny from her earlier time on the dance floor, even though Hunter seemed to be eyeing the glimpse of her shoulder the black dress afforded. *Finally realizing I'm not eleven years old anymore?* Amelie thought with satisfaction.

"Here I was, thinking you'd stayed in for the night," Amelie said, hoping she sounded teasing, and not like she'd been anxiously awaiting his arrival.

Hunter laughed. "No, just got stuck at Hyde longer than I'd planned."

Amelie had a brief flash of Hunter surrounded by a bevy of Hyde beauties but quickly pushed the jealous thought from her head. Hunter held up his cocktail glass.

"I'm all out—want to have a drink with me?" He held up a finger to the waitress in a short brown minidress and white go-go boots. She waited patiently a few feet away, sizing up both Hunter and Amelie.

"Whatever you're having," Amelie said, liking the easy way the words rolled off her tongue.

Hunter cocked his head toward the waitress. "Two Bombay and tonics," he said without hesitation. "Put it on my tab."

The waitress smiled and quickly strode off in the direction of the bar.

"So, Amelie Adams, come here often?" Hunter's voice sounded playful as he sat down on the wide banquette seat, patting a spot next to him for Amelie.

She folded herself into the chair, turning just enough that she could see Hunter's face. "It's my first time, actually," she admitted. As Hunter's leg brushed her bare thigh, she reminded herself to thank Kady for the alone time with him.

The waitress returned with their drinks, lowering her white-shadowed eyelids at Hunter. He took a sip of his gin and tonic and Amelie did the same. The drink was strong, and the gin sent a pleasant burn down her throat and into her chest. The warmth radiated from her middle outward, covering her whole body like a blanket. With her second, bigger sip, she felt the tension leave her shoulders and back, as though she'd just had a La Prairie deep-tissue massage. It was her first cocktail. She was accustomed to champagne's fizzy tickle—she'd had celebratory glasses at New Year's and the occasional wrap party. And she'd tried glasses of wine at dinner with her mom, but never had more than a sip or two. This was different. Her body happily vibrated along with the thumping music, the club's spinning, colored lights washing over her like a warm rainbow.

"I like this dress on you," Hunter said, running two fingertips over the sequins near Amelie's neck. "I don't think I've ever seen you wear black. You look like a whole new woman."

Amelie surveyed his face as coolly as she could, even though her heart was beating double time. She wanted to look at him in a way that said, *I think about you constantly and would like nothing better than to be boyfriend and girlfriend, even if it means my virginity and your sexuality are constantly debated in the press, and we frequently read about our impending breakup in* Life & Style.

Instead, she said, "I'm allowed to leave the princess outfit at home once in a while."

Hunter laughed again, a rich, deep laugh. Amelie beamed, feeling like the word "Yay!" was flashing on her forehead. "Let's dance," he said, picking up both their drinks.

What felt like minutes later, Amelie was sweaty and giddy at the center of the dance floor with Kady, DeAndra, the Lacey twins, and Hunter. It was two thirty in the morning but she felt as fresh as if she'd just woken up. Hunter had been just an arm's reach away all night, and had never let her gin and tonic go dry.

Not that that was a good thing. Amelie definitely felt a little woozy, but thanks to the dancing, she'd burned off enough alcohol not to feel drunk.

Now, the go-go-booted waitresses were making final rounds, announcing last call.

"We should get out of here before we're stuck with all the closers," Kady yelled over Blondie's "One Way or Another."

Amelie nodded, following Kady off the dance floor.

Hunter was right behind them as they made it out onto the street, to waiting taxis and town cars. Kady, DeAndra, and the twins took turns hugging Hunter goodbye, until just Amelie was left standing in front of him.

"This was fun," he said, a bead of sweat on his cheekbone. "You should come out tomorrow night. There's a party at this mansion in the Hollywood Hills. Lewis Buford's place. Have you heard of him?"

Amelie shook her head, pulling her straightened red hair off her neck as she did so.

"Well, you don't need to know him. I'm inviting you. So come, if you want." With that, Hunter reached down and enfolded her in his strong arms. It was all Amelie could do not to run her hands down his solid back. As he let go, Hunter leaned down and kissed her on the cheek.

Without even thinking about her schedule or if she'd be too tired, she beamed back at Hunter. "I'll be there."

At ten thirty the next morning, Amelie strode through the door of the two-story Craftsman she and her mom had purchased in Toluca Lake the previous year. Though it wasn't original by any means, having been built in the 1990s and not the 1890s, they'd both fallen in love with the expanse of white-railed patio on the red house's frame.

Amelie was still wearing the yoga pants and *Class Angel* production T-shirt she'd slept in the night before.

Well, barely slept in. Amelie's night had been one of a happy insomniac as she replayed all of her and Hunter's moments like some kind of glorious dream.

The only not-so-great thing was that she'd missed call time for the Kidz Network promos she was supposed to do. But she'd at least called to cancel and ask for a reschedule. She'd gone to Fairy Princess shoots sick as a dog. So this was just like comp time, she rationalized.

She woke up with no sign of a hangover and now practically bounced on her Ugg-covered feet into the house. She passed through what was once their unused dining room, now a shared office for her and her mom. A chandelier hung in its center, and each side of the room contained a matching oak desk with wing-backed chairs upholstered in a shiny pink leaf pattern. Her mom's desk was spare, with room for her laptop, a vertical file sorter containing several folders, copies of today's *Hollywood Reporter* and *Variety*, and an old-fashioned-looking phone. Amelie's desk contained a pile of scripts, some scattered across the desk's wide surface, a white iMac with a twenty-four-inch monitor, and a Fairy Princess doll that had fallen on its side next to her two-foot stack of fashion magazines.

Amelie skipped into the kitchen, an airy room with sunny yellow mosaic tiles along the walls, cream granite countertops, and hand-carved oak cabinets. In the car on the way over, she'd rehearsed her speech about all the fun she and Kady had had, if her mom asked. Natalie Portman movie. Mani-pedis. Et cetera. Her mom was sitting at the breakfast bar, her laptop open in front of her and an oversize mug of coffee at her side.

Helen looked up from the computer, her face set in an irritated frown, without a trace of welcome for her daughter.

"Morning, Mom," Amelie chirped, heading to the Cuisinart coffeepot to pour herself a mug. Most likely, Helen was just getting worked up over something on the *Huffington Post*. "What's wrong in the world today?"

Helen sighed. "I don't know where to begin." She turned the MacBook Air so that the screen was facing Amelie. Instantly, Amelie recognized the garish red lettering of the TMZ home page. On the front page was a fuzzy, camera phone photo—unmistakably Amelie and Hunter, bathed in Area's rainbow lights. Hunter clutched a drink in his hand and was grinning at Amelie. Amelie had both arms in the air, and a cocktail in her right hand. Beneath the photo was a simple headline, "Fairy Prudeness No More?" Amelie skimmed the text of the story beneath it.

> Adams, best known as Fairy Princess—the goodiest good girl ever—is a never-seen on the L.A. club circuit, so her ease in tossing back cocktails and seducing in-demand Sparks is sure to be big news to her fans, not to mention Kidz Network, which has praised its progeny for her clean-living ways.

Helen pursed her lips. "As your manager, I can't tell you how bad a light this casts you in." She closed the laptop before Amelie could read the rest of the story. "As your mother, I can't believe you lied to me. I'm sad to say I've tacked this to the Board. You're grounded. Please go to your room now."

Shame washed over Amelie as she took one long last look at her carefree face in the TMZ photo. She padded out of the kitchen and up the oak staircase to her room.

Her mom was right. Now that Amelie really thought about it, she couldn't believe how easily she'd canceled her appointment this morning. How carelessly she'd stood up Jake. She cringed, imagining Kidz Network president Dan Davies—who'd always been her biggest fan—seeing the photo. *I can't believe I did that,* she thought, stopping on the fourth stair and staring at a photo of her nine-year-old self in full Fairy Princess regalia. The tabloids would have a field day with her. What if she lost everything? She knew the time was drawing closer when she'd need a post–Fairy Princess career, but she'd always imagined her departure would be on her own terms. Had she just thrown away her good reputation?

Reaching her bedroom, with its vaulted ceilings, hardwood floors, and a nook for studying and reading, Amelie flopped down on her four-poster bed. It was the bed she'd always wanted as a child. Her mom had had it custom-made after Amelie's first *Fairy Princess* paycheck arrived.

She stared up at the white lace canopy, the sick feeling of guilt bubbling in her stomach. She wished she could erase the night before. Her mom was mad at her. Dan Davies was probably mad at her. Her fans' parents were probably lighting up the web with nasty comments about how disappointed they were that their kids' role model had proved to be just another bad influence.

This is what I get for being good all this time, Amelie thought. *If I hadn't been on my "I'm better than everyone" high horse, it would be no big deal now if I got spotted drinking at a club. With Hunter Sparks.*

But that was true: She was sixteen years old, not twelve. Wasn't she long overdue to sneak out and do something that pissed off the adults in her life? Wasn't it her right to get into the kind of trouble sixteen-year-olds everywhere else in the country did? Wasn't one night at Area the same as if she went to some wild house party? She hadn't driven home drunk. She hadn't hurt anyone. So she was guilty of a little underage drinking. Weren't, like, 90 percent of girls her age guilty of the same thing? The little girls who watched her show didn't care—or probably even *know*—that Amelie had had three gin and tonics and stayed out until 3 a.m. Or flirted with Hunter.

She smirked in spite of herself. He'd finally asked her out. He could easily have any girl in a twenty-mile radius, and he'd invited *her*. But she was grounded. Banished to her ivory tower. Those twenty-mile-radius girls were going to have a field day at tomorrow's big party. Hunter would probably forget all about her.

Amelie knew she was being childish, lying there feeling sorry for herself. But to her, clubbing was a means to an end: Hunter. She would fully relinquish any partying opportunities once she and he were a solid It couple.

If she didn't go, Hunter would think she was a baby all over again. Or worse, think she didn't like him and had stood him up. Amelie couldn't bear the thought of Hunter waiting for her at Lewis Buford's house, wondering why she hadn't shown up. She *had* to go to that party.

Hearing footfalls on the staircase, Amelie rolled over.

Her mom's voice scolded her through the door. "Also, you left your calendar open on your computer, and I saw you missed tutoring," Helen said sharply. "Call Jacob immediately, apologize, and reschedule."

So much for growing up. Amelie rolled back to her stomach, burying her face in a down pillow. Her perfect night out had officially become a pity party.

ENEMIES CLOSER

"Do you want your nails the same color as your toes?" Tracy, Myla's favorite manicurist at Paint Shop, wiggled the bottle of Dior Vernis Golden Nugget under Myla's nose.

"Please." Myla nodded as Tracy began massaging Myla's hands and wrists with the shop's green tea lotion. Myla leaned back in her chair, half closing her eyes. The narrow salon's line of overhead lights cast their gentle glow on her face. The Pierces' haunting, spooky vocals drifted through the shop, at once girly and ghostly. Myla had provided the sound track—she needed to wallow a little bit, and didn't think she could handle Paint Shop's usual upbeat playlist.

On either side of Myla sat Billie and Talia, also in the midst of manicures. Fortune was absent due to a bad bout of swimmer's ear. She'd also missed the pool party. Not that anyone really minded—Fortune was sweet, but she could be a little much sometimes. The three girls were the only people in the tiny shop on Robertson. Myla had called ahead and paid to have the salon reserved for two hours so she and her friends could enjoy girl talk in private. Paint Shop sometimes overflowed with customers from the Valley who drove down in hopes of spotting regulars like Kate Beckinsale and Gwen Stefani.

Myla opened her eyes, stretching her neck from side to side. On her left, Billie was getting her nails painted in Calvin Klein's Bombshell. Talia had chosen the same shade as Myla. Normally, this would have bothered her, but today she had bigger things on her mind.

"I still don't understand how they even met," Myla said again. She'd been complaining about Ash and Jojo all day at school, the whole ride to the nail salon, and in dozens of text messages to her friends, all with variations on the same note: Do u think they r 2-gether? Jojo + Ash = bad couple rt? and Did A seem ☺ in class 2-day?

What she'd left out was her hurt over Lailah taking Jojo shopping. Myla always resisted Lailah's offers of mother-daughter time because, unlike Jojo, she had friends and a life. But when she'd seen the way Jojo and their mother kissed goodbye this morning, Lailah smoothing her genetic daughter's hair, an act like something off a Mother's Day card, Myla had felt envy rise inside her. And it wasn't just because Jojo looked dazzling in a white and black Rag & Bone pleated minidress with the silver Hollywould wedges she seemed to wear everywhere.

Talia was looking at her matter-of-factly, her blunt-cut hair sleeker than ever thanks to Myla's suggestion of a trim and color-deepening wash at Maxime. "Maybe they have a class together and got assigned to some project together. Or maybe he just noticed her in the hallway. Maybe you should have let her hang out with us, just to keep an eye on her, you know? That whole enemies-closer thing?"

Myla scowled at Talia, knowing she was right but irritated that she had the guts to say such things. "An enemy should be worthy of me. Jojo's a nobody from Sacramento."

On the other side of Myla, Billie played dumb. It wasn't difficult. "I don't know, My. Maybe you should be nicer to her. Like fake nicer. She could hang out with us and then she won't have time to hang out with Ash. At least she's dressing better now. I liked what she had on today." Billie shrugged, wriggling her red Bombshell-clad fingers. For a girl acing precalc, Billie was easily distracted by shiny things.

Yeah, because my mom picked it out, Myla thought, her hands tensing.

"Relax your hand," Tracy commanded. Myla tried to loosen up.

"That's not a bad idea, Myla," Talia piped up, leaning back as Sandra, her preferred manicurist, started painting on a topcoat. "The fake-nice thing."

"Out. Of. The. Question." Myla balled up the fist that Tracy wasn't working on, smearing the still-wet topcoat.

Tracy shook her head, picking up Myla's ruined hand and dabbing off the topcoat with nail polish remover. "This is Ash?" Tracy piped in. "Your boyfriend who used to wait here while you got manicures?"

Myla nodded, remembering how nice it was to have Ash around to find her credit card, carry her purse, and open doors for her when her nails were still drying. She didn't exactly enjoy playing damsel in distress, but Ash made feeling helpless fun.

"Then you can't get so upset over every little thing," Tracy said, kneading Myla's hand once more. She looked sagely at Talia and Billie, who were nodding vigorously. "You're going to see the guy everywhere."

An image of Ash and Jojo together came unbidden into Myla's head. They were standing on stage at BHH's junior prom. Ash looked dashing in a tux, and Jojo wore the beautiful white Oscar de la Renta Lailah had worn to the Oscars last year. They were being crowned king and queen as the whole school burst into applause. Lailah and Barkley were in the crowd, beaming at Jojo. Myla had imagined the moment before—but it had always starred her and Ash. Now, she saw herself alone and dejected in the corner.

She shook off the nightmarish vision. "At school, fine, I have to see him. Maybe I have to bump into him at the Beverly Center or the Grove. But certain things are off-limits. He shouldn't be in my house. He shouldn't be at parties with my friends."

Talia looked down at her golden nails, which looked better than Myla's. "Thank God he's not invited to Lewis's tomorrow," she mumbled.

Myla paused mid-rant. She'd almost forgotten about Lewis Buford's annual school year kickoff bash. It was true: Ash would never show up at Lewis's house. Unless . . .

"Tracy, take out my iPhone," she commanded.

The manicurist pulled the iPhone from Myla's rhinestone scorpion–emblazoned oversize Thomas Wylde lambskin bag, which she'd purchased at Barneys after school that day as a pick-me-up.

"Okay," Myla chirped excitedly. "At the top of my in-box, there's a party invite."

Tracy tapped on the screen a few times. "From Lewis Buford?"

"That's the one." Myla nodded, spinning around once in her chair like a kid at Disneyland. "Go into contacts." "Okay . . ." Tracy did as she was told. In Beverly Hills, dialing cell phones and sending texts was pretty much part of a manicurist's job.

"Now find Ash Gilmour and forward the invite. Add this message: '*Think we should talk. I'm going to be here tomorrow night. See you there?*'"

Talia, Billie, and Tracy exchanged puzzled looks, probably wondering if the smell of nail polish remover was getting to Myla.

Wondering why she hadn't thought of this sooner, Myla let out a contented sigh and stretched in her chair, feeling more relaxed than she had all day. Who needed a foot massage when you could have revenge?

DAYS OF WHINE AND POSERS

"Gilmour, check this out." Ash's friend Tucker pulled a record from Amoeba Music's expansive vinyl selection.

Ash had been dazedly staring at the cover of a crappy used Billy Ocean album. He squinted at the album Tucker was holding, a copy of "Eucalyptus," the Deadly Syndrome's hard-to-find seven-inch single. "Thanks, man." He took the single from Tucker and kept moving down the aisle.

Ash couldn't have lived without his weekly trips to Amoeba, possibly the best music store on earth. Sure, iTunes was easier. But true music junkies needed the physicality of collecting, and no MP3 store ever had the obscure, small record runs that Ash craved.

Located next to the ArcLight Cinema in Hollywood, the cavernous two-story store overflowed with good music. He could find his favorite bands' stuff alongside new albums from groups unknown even to the son of a legendary music producer. Going there always pumped Ash up about re-forming a band. On the way home from every trip, he and Tucker inevitably talked about their future group's vibe.

He'd barely made it from the *O*'s to the *D*'s when
a lanky man-giant who looked like Moby on stilts
approached. His Amoeba name badge read TREV.

"Sweet find." He nodded at the Deadly Syndrome
record under Ash's arm.

Inwardly, Ash rolled his eyes. Trev stared down at
him hopefully. "So, um, have you heard of this new band,
Skybuster?"

Ash suppressed the urge to tell the guy to fuck off.
Normally, he would have played along. Skybuster was
almost certainly the name of Trev's lame band, and Trev,
like dozens of Amoeba clerks before him, had recognized
Ash as Gordon Gilmour's son. Since pretty much every
Amoeba worker was either in a band, managing a band,
or wanting to start a band, Gordon's history with Zeppelin and the Who—not to mention his more recent work
with everyone from Jack White to the Kings of Leon—
was enough to get their vintage hipster panties in a bunch.
The register lines were typically long, and Ash always
waited with a mega-stack of CDs and vinyl. It amused
him to watch the four or five cashiers working the regis-
ters speed up their "too cool to rush" record store clerk
act in hopes of waiting on Ash. In the rare case that the
clerk was new or didn't recognize him, Ash needed only
to slide over his black AmEx for said cashier to suddenly
drop his snooty, "my music is better than yours" disdain
to ask if Ash needed anything else that day. It was like
they all hoped he'd say, *Yeah, my dad's looking for the next
big thing, and I think you're it. Come with me.*

Though he hated to admit it, shopping at Amoeba was
one of the few times Ash appreciated his father, or at least

being his father's son. He wasn't a jerk or anything, but who wouldn't enjoy getting fawned over by guys who made acting blasé their life's mission?

Ash craned his neck to look at Trev eye-to-bloodshot-eye. "Skybuster? That's sort of a lame name."

Trev seemed to shrink at the insult. "Oh, yeah, totally," he sycophantically agreed. "Um, let me know if I can help you find anything else, Mr. Gilmour."

Ash felt a little bad, but he needed some amusement out of this trip. Usually after buying new albums at Amoeba, he'd go home and make Myla a fresh iMix of all the best songs. It was fun to play DJ for her. But today, he'd just go home and listen to music alone, feeling sorry for himself. Even kiss-assy clerks couldn't change that sad fact.

He languidly added the Deadly Syndrome record to his stack—today comprising nothing but the self-pitying kinds of music Ash loved to hate. He would definitely be playing "Eucalyptus," with its "Goodbye, goodbye" chorus, over and over again.

Ash shuffled from the vinyl section into the main CD area, which was at least the size of the BHH gymnasium. He walked right into a super-thin girl in skintight Levis and beat-up royal blue Chuck Taylors. She wore thick black glasses that tried to say, "I don't care if men find me attractive," even if her tight American Apparel V-neck said otherwise. She had a blue streak painted on the underside of her hair, just like the green one Myla had clipped out yesterday.

"Excuse you," she murmured, more teasing than angry. Her breath smelled strongly of clove cigarettes, and she clutched a French import of the Stones' *Exile on Main Street*—Ash's favorite album of all time—to her chest.

She was undeniably sexy, and yet . . . Ash couldn't be bothered.

He stepped off to the side, muttering a quick apology and barely looking up from his John Varvatos black Converse.

The thing was, all the girl did was remind him of Myla. He thought back to a day two summers ago, when she'd forgotten her iPod on a trip to Venice Beach. Lying in the sand next to her, Ash had given up one of his earbuds and they'd listened to all of *Exile* together. Myla had made him play the tenth track, "Happy," over and over again and then had sung the refrain the whole way home: "I need a love to keep me happy / Baby, baby, keep me happy."

He'd never thought that he'd go from keeping her happy to using her new sister to piss her off. Not that he hadn't had a good time with Jojo. She was awesome. But the motives behind their Wii session were less than pure, on both sides.

He'd spent so much time and energy being angry at Myla, but after seeing the hurt look on her face in Jojo's room, all his anger had left him like a balloon losing helium. With the anger gone, he could face his real feelings. He missed her, pure and simple.

Ash glanced around the store, watching clusters of music fans flip through the stacks. The place drew everyone, from twelve- and thirteen-year-olds whose parents had dropped them off at the ArcLight, searching for the kind of music that would be most offensive to their elders, to older music fans who'd never heard of iTunes. They wandered through the big-band and Motown sections, picking up Charlie Parker and Temptations records. And then, of course, no independent music store was complete without the hipster contingent: The humongous store was dotted with dirty-haired guys and carefully bedheaded girls who descended on the place every day like some moody field trip out of Silver Lake.

Ash was ready to get home and start his lonesome listening party. Tucker was no longer in the vinyl section, so Ash scanned the store. It was impossible to pick Tucker's distressed jeans and ironic T-shirt out from those of the seemingly dozens of guys with similar styles hunched over CDs in the bowling alley–length aisles.

He leaned back against the wall, deciding to wait for Tucker to find him. The Italian version of a *Ghostbusters* poster wrinkled beneath the weight of his back. Whatever, he'd pay for it.

Just then his iPhone vibrated in his pocket. Digging past a crumpled homework assignment, Ash saw he had an e-mail. Probably some lame photo Geoff had taken with a chick he just met at the Santa Monica Promenade. Geoff kept inviting Ash on tail-hunting missions, but Ash had zero energy for that kind of thing.

Ash's heart beat faster. The e-mail was from *Myla*.

"Think we should talk. I'm going to be here tomorrow night. See you there?"

An invite to a huge party. At . . . Lewis Buford's house. Okay, fine, he hated that guy more than Beatles fans hated Yoko Ono. But Myla wanted him there. She wanted to see him, wanted to talk. She wanted to—he knew what she wanted. She wanted to get back together.

Nothing would stop him from being at that party.

A goofy grin broke out on Ash's face. Feeling more alive than he had all week, Ash wove his way to the *P* section, looking for the '70s band Peaches & Herb.

He dumped his pile of self-pity music on the end of a counter. He didn't need it anymore. Right now, he couldn't get the Peaches & Herb song out of his head and sang it to himself. "Reunited—and it feels so good!"

FASHION DENIM

"Is your steak okay?" Amelie glanced nervously at Jake. He had barely taken two bites of his New York strip.

He'd sounded a little distant on the phone when she'd called him to apologize this morning, but at least he'd agreed to meet her for a makeup tutoring session at eat. on sunset. The restaurant was actually not on Sunset Boulevard, but on Gower Street, and Amelie had felt odd trying to explain the idiosyncratic location to Jake.

Jake nodded. "Yeah, absolutely," he said, cutting into the medium-rare meat and chewing on a big bite.

It was six o'clock, still early on Friday evening, and the restaurant's patio was practically empty. Jake and Amelie sat in slatted-back chairs on opposite sides of a wide cherrywood outdoor table. Behind each of them stood a tall propane heater—an L.A. restaurant must-have if you wanted to fill your patio with thin (and thin-skinned) starlets on the city's chilly evenings. The night was cool, and Amelie rubbed her arms beneath her Splendid rugby cardigan, wishing she'd worn another layer.

"So, thanks for meeting me," Amelie said, as she

thoughtfully prodded an asparagus spear and a ricotta gnocchi onto her fork. "I'm really, really sorry about yesterday."

Jake dipped a fry into his béarnaise sauce. "It's no big deal," he said. "I know you're busy."

Jake chewed carefully, trying not to say more than he needed to. He knew Amelie had been out last night with some girls from her movie and Hunter Sparks. The buzz was all over school. Supposedly, BHH's newspaper editor, a senior who thought he was the next Perez Hilton, had snapped the photo that wound up on TMZ. Jake felt protective of Amelie, even though he was only her tutor. He'd wanted to punch that meathead Rod Stegerson, who he'd heard trashing Amelie in the halls: *Dude, Fairy Princess is a skank! But I'd tap that anyway.*

Now he just felt awkward. He stared at the curl of Amelie's red hair as it fell against her creamy skin, not knowing what to talk about. She'd asked him about the Dodgers—who he knew sucked this year—and L.A.'s two basketball teams, who hadn't even started their season. If she was looking for a guy who knew all the preseason buzz, he wasn't it. He also felt self-conscious in his new clothes: A striped bamboo cotton hoodie and these crazy organic Rogan jeans—fashion denim, as Miles kept saying. The jeans were cool and all, but the scratchy organic denim felt like he was wearing a bunch of paper towels stitched together into pants.

Amelie pushed a stalk of asparagus around her plate, trying to think of something to say. She had offered to treat Jake for dinner, and now she wanted to make sure he had a good time. She was trying her best to get Jake talking, running through every L.A. sports team she could name. He'd barely answered and seemed distracted as he fiddled with the zipper on his navy blue and orange hoodie. It must have been brand-new, as it still bore the perfect crease marks of a store's display.

This outing had to go well. Amelie's mom was in full-on Protective Momager mode. When Amelie said she was planning to meet Jake for a makeup tutoring session, Helen had insisted on driving her to the restaurant, and even walked in with her. Now her mom was at the Beverly Center, shopping as she waited to pick up Amelie. Amelie was worried she'd never have any freedom again. It was like her mom had volunteered to chaperone the prom.

She leaned across the table, spearing one of Jake's truffle fries with her fork and biting off its crispy end playfully. "New sweatshirt?" She gestured with her fork at Jake's pristine hoodie. "It looks good on you."

Jake, who'd been sitting as straight as a wooden puppet, seemed to loosen with relief. He grinned widely. "Thanks," he said, proudly smoothing the shirt's front. "I found it at Kitson today. It's Great China Wall or something."

She cocked her head to one side, blowing back the strand of red hair that fell across her cheekbone. "So I was wondering what you're doing tomorrow night."

Jake suddenly straightened in his chair again. "Um, nothing great has come to mind, you know, yet."

"Would you want to go with me to this party, in the Hollywood Hills? Pick me up at maybe nine?" She flashed her best "please do this for me" grin.

It was simple: The only way out of her house was if she told her mom she had a tutoring session. All other options were impossible—her mom was watching her like a hawk, and as Amelie's manager, she knew Amelie didn't have to report to the set tomorrow. Jake was Amelie's only hope, a realization she'd had during her pity party late last night. Amelie looked across the table at him, feeling impatient to hear his answer.

She felt bad, knowing she'd kind of be using him to go to the party. But maybe he'd meet a cute girl, one who was good at geometry or something. And she'd finally land Hunter, once and for all. They could double-date, Amelie decided, the fantasy growing in her head. It would probably be good for Hunter to be around more down-to-earth, normal guys like Jake. Jake commanded himself to hold it together, the words repeating on a loop in his head. *Party. Hollywood Hills. Pick me up at nine. Pick me up at nine.* He adjusted his focus so that he was staring at the fourteenth brick from the top in the section of wall directly behind Amelie's shoulder.

He'd thought Miles was an idiot, leading him around Kitson as the salesgirls gave them dirty looks. But the fashion denim had worked! One second, he was feeling like the biggest loser in the world, trying to remember whatever his little brother had said about the Dodgers catcher Russell Martin at dinner last night. The next, she was asking him to a party. The words *Kitson* and *Great China Wall* were practically magic.

Yes, he'd be brown-bagging lunch to afford gas for the Corolla for a while, but it was worth it. It was like those commercials:

Tight skull T-shirt your friend Miles says is *so now*: $90.

Hoodie that makes you look like a trendy version of Bert from *Sesame Street*: $250.

Jeans with some third-world country's flag sewn on the back pocket: $220.

A date with Amelie Adams: Priceless.

"That sounds great," he said, popping a French fry in his mouth. It was the first one he'd been able to taste since he arrived. "I'll pick you up then."

FLOCK OF SEGALS

"Gwyneth would like two of every piece in the new Wyeth line, one in a size two and one in a size four."

Jojo glanced up from pretending to examine a bracelet that promised instant Zen for $175. The speaker was a tiny brunette in a smock dress that would have been conservative, save for its mid-thigh hem and off-the-shoulder neckline. The woman poked the keys of her BlackBerry, probably to let Gwyneth know she'd secured her quarry. Or to e-mail a tabloid and inform them that Gwynnie was shopping for both her bloated *and* her skinny days.

Jojo was shopping at Fred Segal on Melrose. It had taken the better part of her trigonometry class to decide if she should go to the famous store's West Hollywood or Santa Monica location. Santa Monica's was way bigger—it was built on the site of a former ice rink—but rumor had it that stars preferred the older, smaller location on Melrose, even though it was no longer even owned by the Segal family. It had also taken her an hour to decide on what to wear shopping at such an exclusive store, this time without Lailah at her side. She'd chosen a gray Miu Miu bow-belted cardigan over a navy C&C California scoop-neck tank, paired with a gray and blue pin-striped Nanette Lepore pleated miniskirt and navy Prada kidskin Mary Janes. Every other customer, she noticed, seemed to be wearing jeans.

"Oh, and add a few Ella Moss tops, whatever's newest, for Kate, but no pink," the stylist said, never looking up from her PDA. The salesgirl didn't scurry off at the mention of top-tier clientele. Instead, she nodded coolly, adjusting the strap of her Lotta Stensson peacock-print minidress. She strode out of view, presumably to assemble the purchases.

Jojo was shopping for tomorrow night's party in the Hollywood Hills. Despite the closet full of new clothes she'd purchased with Lailah this week, she felt like she needed to select something even more special for her first real BHH party. It was at Lewis Buford's house, which had been the backdrop for a New Year's Eve edition of *The Hills* last year, and Jojo remembered it as utterly fabulous. Myla had actually invited her to the big shindig, after some not-so-subtle prompting from Lailah.

Jojo wasn't going to let Myla's presence stop her from going. Even if Myla planned to get to the party and immediately abandon her, Jojo knew it wouldn't be another Beverly Hills Hotel pool party fiasco. On the car ride over to Fred Segal, she'd texted Ash to see if he was going and he had responded, u know it. ;-). Jojo had stared at his winky-faced emoticon the whole rest of the ride, her heart beating fast.

In part, Jojo's outfit hunt was about finding something

Ash-friendly. Or maybe Ash-*boyfriend*ly. After they'd hung out the other day, Jojo couldn't deny it: She had a crush. But, unlike her unrequited love for Justin Klatch back in Sacramento, she was already on speaking terms with Ash, and he was giving her lots of positive reinforcement. He'd texted her this morning to say he'd had fun hanging out. Then she'd bumped into him while walking past his locker and he'd introduced her to his friend Tucker, who'd been really friendly. Jojo had been on a high all day, imagining Ash telling his friends about her.

She felt a little lost in Fred Segal, having spent an hour cycling through its various boutiques. The store was a labyrinth of fashion, and the three- to four-digit price tags still made her heart skip a beat—but Barbar had insisted their money was her money. And so was their black AmEx. Every clothing line had its own area, and the store was divided into separate boutiques for couture, more casual separates, denim, accessories, and beauty products. Fabrics of every texture and hue called out to Jojo. She was carrying several items, including a pair of J Brand jeans, a gorgeous, asymmetrically hemmed blue Jovovich-Hawk silk minidress with a peekaboo slip, Tucker camisoles in aqua and white, and a red cinch-waist tank from a new line by Blake Lively. She felt a little neglected, having been acknowledged by the shopgirls and guys with cool nods but no offers to try anything on.

Jojo eyed a long gold necklace with a crystal owl charm. It would look perfect with either the minidress or jeans and one of the sexy tanks, she decided, as her cell phone trilled with the Mario Kart music. Jojo had changed it after her and Ash's Wii session.

"Hello," she near-whispered, walking into an unpopulated nook of the store. She didn't want to disturb a heated conversation near the sunglasses display. A skinny guy in yellow pants, a purple cashmere sweater-vest, and a matching fedora and a buff guy wearing beat-up jeans and a tight, thin cotton tee with the words *Hate Me* printed on it, were debating whether it had been a bad career move for Matthew McConaughey to take a role in a legal thriller that would require him to wear a shirt at all times.

"Hey, J, what's up?" Willa's familiar voice poured through Jojo's new iPhone. Jojo could hear the theme song from *Chowder*, Willa's little brother's favorite cartoon, in the background.

"Thank God," Jojo squealed, balancing the pile of clothes in her left arm while she held the phone with her right. "You're just the person I wanted to talk to."

"Oh yeah?" Willa sounded surprised. "What's going on? I got your e-mail about Ash, but you didn't answer my question about whether you'd be here for the soccer invitational next weekend."

"I know," Jojo said, wandering past a tiny woman who looked a lot like Nicole Richie with her daughter. "I'll figure it out. But right now, help me decide what to wear to this party. I could go with the sexy jeans and a sort of skimpy but not slutty tank top, or I found this awesome dress that's, like, short but with a slip that kind of hangs out from under the skirt. But I can't decide what Ash might like better." Jojo stopped near a handbag display, biting her lip.

"Couldn't you just buy them all and decide tomorrow?" Willa suggested. "You can always return stuff. That's my policy."

"You're brilliant," Jojo said, bouncing on her heels and almost toppling a row of Kooba purses.

"I know," Willa bragged. "But anyway, did you see my text about the Butt-Nerd? She's on this health kick and we have to keep a three-week *food and feeling* journal. WTF does that have to do with chemistry?"

The Butt-Nerd, or Ms. Budner, was the most eccentric teacher at their Sacramento high school. She taught chemistry, but every school year became obsessed with something new and worked it into the curriculum. Last year, when the Butt-Nerd had been trying to be a screenwriter, her junior chem classes had had to star in her film *Pierre and Marie*, about the Curies. It had aired on Sacramento's cable access station. Now, she'd apparently moved on to nutrition.

Jojo was half listening and half idly walking down the rows of handbags. Her eyes fell on a row of the most gorgeous purses she'd ever seen. Clutches leaned against mini-hobos, which leaned against larger hobo bags, which leaned against oversize totes. At the very center, on a platform by itself, stood a gleaming white deconstructed leather bag with a top flap adorned by golden Swarovski crystals in the shape of a star.

On the platform stood a sign in the same crystals: THE CHAMPAGNE BAG BY MARTIN RITTENHOUSE. Even though she could practically smell the outrageous price tag from where she stood, Jojo had to have it. The bag was the ideal emblem of her new Hollywood life.

Willa was still talking about the Butt-Nerd. ". . . and Aiden Witner walked into class the other day and said the Butt-Nerd was doing downward dog and totally farted in his face."

Jojo was hypnotized by the bag. "Sorry. I have to go. Love you, 'bye."

She pressed end and spun on her new Mary Janes. The salesgirl in the peacock dress had just finished bagging the stylist's orders for Gwynnie and Kate as Jojo approached her.

"Hi, um, miss," Jojo said, not seeing a name tag. "I'm interested in that bag, the Rittenhouse." She pointed toward the exquisite purse.

The peacock girl tilted her head, her blunt-cut bangs hanging in her eyes. She studied the bag as though looking at a bird that might fly away. "You want that bag," she said, in the "I'm so over it" voice of Angeleno fashionistas. "Sorry. There's a two-year waiting list for that bag, and we're holding that one for Reese."

Jojo felt like the girl had just cut off her arm. She looked at the surrounding handbags, none of which called to her the way this gorgeous one did. Her nose twitched in disappointment. *It's just a bag,* she told herself. *And* Reese *wants it. Who am I to think I can have it?*

But then Jojo had an epiphany.

She *was* someone.

Pouting, she made laserlike eye contact with the shopgirl, whose eyelashes were painted with electric blue mascara. "Oh, that's too bad," Jojo said, dropping her shoulders. "I wanted to get it for my mom. She'd look so great with it at Sundance. She has a little indie premiering there. *Left of Nowhere?*"

Sure, *Left of Nowhere,* about a single mom struggling to raise her brilliant but autistic child, wasn't a blockbuster. But *Variety* was already talking Oscar number two for

Lailah. As the title left Jojo's lips, Peacock went from bored to all ears.

"You mean that drama starring Lailah Barton? With the retarded kid?" Blunt Bangs asked, trying to hide her excitement but not doing a great job of it. "Your mom is Lailah Barton?"

Jojo nodded, smiling. Another blond salesgirl in Lohan leggings stopped folding Lauren Moshi tees and walked over, as if Lailah's name had magnetic pull. Two fabulously tall salesgirls who'd been unpacking a box of True Religion jeans followed suit, orbiting Jojo like trendy zombies.

They all eyed the peacock-dress girl with envy. Lailah was known for repaying kindnesses done to her children.

"You're the new kid," Peacock said, a flash of recognition lighting her eyes. "Well, the real kid."

"Yes, that's true," Jojo said, savoring each word like it was the last bite of a delicious, charmed-life cookie.

"Oh, wow, those pictures of you in *In Touch* don't do you justice. I'm Melina by the way." She shook Jojo's hand. "Follow me."

Melina headed in the direction of the Rittenhouse bag and Jojo followed. The legginged shopgirl unloaded the clothes from Jojo's arms and assured her she'd bag them. Then she made a dash for the denim bar, grabbing jeans from the shelves and promising Jojo to pick some other key pieces that would be perfect for her. If Jojo didn't like something or needed a different size, she could just call and they'd messenger over something else. Jojo smiled to herself. This was too easy.

Staring up at the white bag reverently, Melina turned and smiled at Jojo. The guys debating Matthew McConaughey's career fell silent, studying Jojo from behind the racks of designer sunglasses.

"You know, Reese is late picking it up," Peacock said. "It's only fair you get it. From what I know, Martin Rittenhouse idolizes Lailah. Who wouldn't, right?"

"Right," Jojo said, as Melina reached for the bag, her short dress riding up to expose even more thigh. Melina put the bag gently on Jojo's shoulder. She walked Jojo over to a mirror, decorated with twinkle lights and surrounded on each side by fluttery, gem-colored dresses.

"It's actually perfect with your coloring," she complimented Jojo, staring at her in the mirror. Behind them, Jojo could see the other salesgirls folding and refolding the shop's signature tees as they watched the exchange. "Your mom's probably cool enough to let you borrow it."

"She really is," Jojo nodded, pointing at her shoes, which sparkled beneath the store's sunlight-mimicking overhead lights. "She and I are almost the same shoe size, too."

"You're so lucky." Melina sighed. "My mom's still walking around in a 2003 Juicy Couture sweatsuit and Uggs she bought five years ago." She rolled her eyes conspiratorially.

Two hours later, Jojo exited the ivy-covered store onto Melrose Boulevard. Her arms were weighted down with shopping bags brimming with the kind of clothes she'd previously only seen in the pages of glossy magazines.

A group of girls carrying bags from a Melrose store that sold quality knockoffs strolled by, chatting. A brunette at the group's center spotted Jojo and didn't try to hide her stare. She recognized her.

Charlie, the Everharts' driver, pulled up and opened the SUV's freshly waxed door. As Jojo handed him her shopping bags and stepped into the waiting car, she heard the brunette say to her friends, "Do you know who that was? Barbar's daughter Jojo. Their *real* kid. She's, like, Hollywood royalty."

At that moment, Jojo wouldn't have argued.

QUICK-CHANGE ARTIST

Jacob's palms were sweaty against the stems of the bouquet he held at his side. It was his third bouquet purchase of the day from Bristol Farms. His mom had loved his hand-me-down gifts of roses, which he'd decided were a little too much, and an assortment of red carnations that he'd found pretty but which Miles had voted down. "Dude, have you never watched *Sex and the City*? Girls hate carnations, unless they tell you they like them." This was one of the most confusing things Miles had ever said, but then again, he'd been right about the fashion jeans.

So now Jacob stood on Amelie Adams's front porch holding what he hoped was the perfect bouquet: a dozen gerbera daisies in a rainbow of colors. The wooden slats of the porch creaked beneath his new Kenneth Cole dress shoes and he took a breath, working up the nerve to ring the bell. He hoped no member of a Toluca Lake neighborhood watch group thought he was a stalker, skulking in the shadows on Amelie's front steps.

Amelie lived next to the actual Toluca Lake, which few people realized existed. A neighborhood of Los Angeles safely nestled between Burbank and North Hollywood, Toluca Lake was home to lots of stars who wanted to raise their kids away from Beverly Hills and its excesses while still enjoying an aura of exclusivity and luxury. The lake was next to a golf course, but you had to wind down lots of narrow side streets to find it. The hidden-enclave feeling of the location meant homes here were worth millions, even if the surrounding towns were strictly middle class.

He glanced at his Corolla once more, parked on Navajo Street. He'd just washed it, but it still looked scrawny and unworthy to carry around any cute girl, much less Fairy Princess. Between his grandma's old car and the now-sweaty flowers, he wasn't exactly pimping. But Amelie had asked him out, after all.

"Here goes," Jake mumbled to himself, pressing the bell and taking a step back.

The door opened and an older version of Amelie, her eyes a dark hazel, stood in the doorway. She smiled warmly and stepped backwards into the house. "You must be Jacob," she said. "I'm Helen, Amelie's mother."

He extended his hand for her to shake. "It's Jake, actually." Jake grinned excitedly. Amelie must have told her mom all about him.

"Well, come in," Helen said, gesturing inside. "She should be down soon."

Jake stepped into the entryway, which felt pretty homey. In the center was an oak staircase up to the second floor. On one side of the stairs was a living room with a stone fireplace and two matching couches in a light brown material. They framed a coffee table shaped like an old shipping trunk, on which lay a few random magazines. Jake could picture Amelie stretched out on one of the couches, reading a script.

Helen eyed Jake's flowers quizzically, then seemed to examine his outfit. Miles had helped put it together and Jake had to admit, he didn't look half bad. He was wearing a Paul Smith button-down with simple silver cuff links (thanks to a tip in GQ), and a pair of indigo Diesel boot-cut jeans with artfully frayed back pocket detail. Jake had almost been late getting to Amelie's after having to explain to his father why a person would pay extra money for pants that came pre-frayed.

"You really dressed up, hmm, Jake?" Helen sounded so matter-of-fact, Jake didn't know if her question required a response. He was debating whether to nod politely or answer when Amelie emerged from a room at the top of the stairs.

"Hey Jake," she called sunnily. She swung a lumpy L.L. Bean backpack over one shoulder and descended the stairs noisily, her rubber Havaianas flip-flops slapping the wood with each step.

Her red hair hung in loose curls around her face and her cheeks glowed with just a hint of some shimmery makeup. She looked gorgeous as always, but she was wearing her beat-up jeans—actually beat-up, not high-fashion beat-up—and an L.A. Dodgers T-shirt beneath an oversize gray hoodie.

Jake could feel the sweat crawling up his spine beneath his expensive new shirt. Was this party some casual thing? Was he going to look like some *Details*-obsessed douchebag while everyone else walked around in sandals and T-shirts? He should have asked Amelie what kind of party this was. According to Miles, the number one rule of L.A. style was that it was better to be underdressed than overdressed. That way, everyone thought you were too important to bother spending time on your outfit. Jake felt like he'd been punched. He'd violated rule number one before he'd even gotten in the game.

"Hi Amelie," Jake said, as Amelie reached the bottom of the stairs with a cheerful bounce. Jake held out the flowers gingerly. He felt like those were overkill now, too. Thank God he hadn't gone with the roses.

"Oh, um, they were selling these at the gas station. For charity," he lied, brandishing the flowers. "So I got them."

Amelie took the daisies and smelled them, even though they didn't have a scent to speak of. "That's so nice of you, Jake." She thrust them at her mother.

Helen nodded in agreement. "I'll put them in some water. You guys should get going," she said, shooing them toward the door. "Nice meeting you, Jake. Have a good study session!"

Jake fidgeted beneath his fancy shirt. He felt like he was in one of those dreams where you're naked in front of a whole bunch of people. Amelie's mom thought they were studying? They descended the front porch steps and Amelie slowed as they reached the sidewalk. "Which one's you?"

Jacob's Corolla, waxed and polished to within an inch of its life, looked like it could use vitamins compared to the SUVs along the curb. "That's me," he said, jogging in front of her to unlock the door. He held it open for her and she got in, murmuring a compliment on the Corolla's shine.

Jake got in on his side, put the key into the ignition, and pulled carefully away from the curb, trying not to dent the vintage Thunderbird behind him. He turned to Amelie, who was already rifling through her backpack.

"You told your mom we were studying?" He looked sidelong at her as she pulled a shimmery handful of fabric from her backpack.

"She's a little uptight. Overprotective," Amelie said, shaking out what appeared to be a teeny dress covered in emerald green beads. "Now, turn left at Riverside and keep your eyes on the road—and nothing but the road." She giggled, punching him playfully on the arm.

Jake concentrated, turning onto Riverside. Next to him, he heard the sound of Amelie unzipping her hoodie. Out of the corner of his eye, he caught her wriggling out of it. Then she reached under the oversize Dodgers tee and unbuttoned her jeans as she kicked off her flip-flops.

"Take this to Cahuenga and turn left," Amelie commanded. Jake stared straight ahead, as an old man wearing an overcoat and a knitted cap rolled his shopping cart across the intersection in front of Bob's Big Boy.

He heard the sound of Amelie's jeans unzipping. He suppressed a gulp. Then he heard the denim fabric sliding over her skin as she removed her pants. Jake continued to stare straight ahead, even though his peripheral vision kept picking up the tops of Amelie's thighs, the bright blue cotton of her T-shirt cutting a line across them.

Fairy Princess, hot Fairy Princess, is half naked in my passenger seat, Jake thought, blood rushing to places he didn't want it to rush to right now. If she took off one more item of clothing, he was going to crash the car.

He zoomed his focus in on the taillights of the Beamer in front of him.

He was glad when he reached a red light on Cahuenga. He stared at it intently, like he was taking an eye test. He had to. It was that moment that Amelie chose to quickly pull her shirt off, before even more swiftly dropping the green shimmery dress over her head.

Thank God for red lights, he thought. If he hadn't been stopped, he would definitely have careened right into the 7-Eleven across the street, totaling his Corolla.

The thing was, with the world's most gorgeous redhead undressing just inches from him, he was really starting to like this car.

OF FOOLS AND TOOLES

"Don't forget to stop by the tennis courts, everyone. There's beer, top-shelf liquor, a bonfire, and a live set by Goodbar—with a special guest performance from your host, Lewis Buford!"

Barnsley Toole, Lewis Buford's number one ass-kisser, was standing atop a bar stool at the center of Lewis's rec room, one of the mansion's forty-plus rooms (not including bathrooms, of course). The overhead lights danced on his shiny, effeminate blond hair, and made the orange Brooks Brothers cashmere sweater tied around his neck look baby girl pink. He'd gone overboard on the preppy pastels, and wore pale yellow pants with tiny blue whales on them. Barnsley was even more annoying in person than when he appeared in the pages of *Us Weekly*, which he inevitably did, spreading rumors about up-and-coming starlets one week and hooking up with them by the next week's issue. A few months ago, he kept popping up on *The Hills*, tagging along with Heidi and Spencer. Apparently sick of not having the spotlight to himself, he'd convinced MTV to give him a show, *Barnsley's Babes*. Now cameras followed him from club to party as he hit on unsuspecting girls. For right now, at least, female party guests were avoiding him. Barnsley was legendary for getting girls drunk so that he'd never have an episode where he struck out. Tonight, a cameraman was tracking Barnsley's every move, fully expecting him to get some action.

The Everharts' driver had dropped Myla and Jojo off in the massive U-shaped driveway half an hour ago, and Myla had promptly ditched Jojo. But that wasn't really a bad thing. Jojo had done a self-tour of the house's main floor, winding her way through a living room with a real Picasso and an Elton John piano, a dining room with Wedgwood place settings for twenty-four, and a kitchen with a Sub-Zero refrigerator that spanned an entire wall.

Jojo thought back to what she'd been doing this weekend of last school year: Sitting at a booth in Sadie's Pizza with the girls' soccer team, drinking pitchers of Diet Coke and sharing a pepperoni pie while taking turns flirting with the one cute waiter.

Now she was sitting on a comfortable spinning stool at the bar in the Bufords' rec room. By itself, the room was nearly the size of Sadie's Pizza. It felt like an English pub, with a dark mahogany bar that matched the paneled walls. Overhead, Tiffany lamps—each with an English ivy pattern surrounding a stained glass letter *B* at the center—dangled from chains, casting dim glows over the bar and the various play areas. With its dartboards, pool table, foosball game, air hockey, and even chess table, the room was like Chuck E. Cheese for adults. In the corner, a guy from NBC's new reality show *Underground* was making out with the blonde who'd recently been sent home on *The Bachelor*.

The red felt-covered pool table was at the room's center, and Jojo recognized a few of Ash's friends: Tucker, whom she'd met, and—was it Geoff?—playing a game with Billie and Talia, who'd supposedly taken Myla's side in the breakup. *So much for that*. Jojo chuckled to herself.

Even though she was sitting at the bar alone, she felt perfectly comfortable. Some cute surfer-type dudes were working the bar, and one of them had been consistently refilling her amaretto stone sour and giving her extra maraschino cherries with each top-off. She was feeling good, in a warm, fuzzy, slightly tipsy way. It helped that she'd put together the ultimate outfit.

Even Myla had looked at her with a glint of jealousy. Jojo carried her new bag, of course. She couldn't resist sashaying in her fluttery celestial-blue Jovovich-Hawk dress, the wispy peekaboo slip beneath the short petal-like skirt tickling her legs as she did so. Her owl pendant dangled onto the dress's neckline, and her suede Tod's wedge sandals in periwinkle—Lailah had picked them up at Barneys during a shopping trip this week—were actually comfortable. It was the kind of slightly edgy, piecemeal outfit she'd seen Myla pull off countless times in the tabloids. Her shoulders were bare, showing the last vestiges of her summer tan. More than once, guys she recognized from school had given her nods of acknowledgment, even appreciation.

Cocking her head to signal the bartender, Jojo felt like she'd been hanging out at Lewis Buford's house her whole life.

The cute bartender presented her with another stone sour. Her third? Or fourth? He winked, and Jojo smiled coyly in return. She took a long sip from her thin red straw and spun back to face the room, hoping to see Ash. Some of the party guests had lit cigars, and the sickly sweet smoke hung like a haze in front of her. Barnsley Toole kept slinking by, telling people they could head outside to swim or catch the band. He'd paid two visits to Jojo, paying compliments on her legs. Both times, she'd given him "get lost" eye rolls. He looked like a flat-faced blond cat. Jojo giggled to herself, imagining him licking his paws. She felt sorry for whoever was dumb enough to make out with him tonight.

If she made out with anyone tonight, it would be Ash, Jojo thought, enjoying the candy-flavored drink as it warmed her from the inside out. She'd texted to see if he was on his way, but had gotten no answer. If she'd known his friends a little better, she'd have asked them, but there was the added no-no factor of Myla's friends lurking close by.

A few more people slipped through the sliding double doors that led from the kitchen to the rec room. Jojo recognized runners-up from both *American Idol* and *America's Next Top Model*, and . . . Ash.

He stood in the doorway for a second, looking adorable in a rumpled button-down, slightly baggy Diesel jeans, and his beat-up Vans. He pushed back the strand of dirty blond hair falling messily in his face, and then his eyes landed on her. He smiled slowly.

Jojo's heart was pounding in her chest. Sure, it was a bad idea to make a play for Ash. No, a terrible idea. She was on rocky enough ground with Myla, and hooking up with Ash was sure to bring on a full-fledged avalanche. But whatever. It wasn't like Myla was making huge efforts at sisterly bonding . . . or even peace.

"Jojo, looking good," Ash said, sounding like he'd had a few drinks himself. "Come here often?" His eyes twinkled at his lame joke.

Jojo shrugged flirtatiously. "Oh, you know me, I never miss a party in the Hills." She knew it wasn't her best material, but under the circumstances, not to mention the influence, it was the best she could come up with.

Ash sank onto the empty bar stool next to her. "Well, I gotta tell you, the guy who owns this place? Total tool. He doesn't deserve someone as hot as you as a party guest."

Jojo watched an ice cube melt in her drink, her cheeks burning. Ash had just called her hot. He was leaning close, so close she could smell his soap—something cucumber-y and clean—and feel the warmth of his breath.

"I know," Jojo said, attempting a sexy whisper. "But I'm not really here for him." *I'm here for you*, she willed Ash to realize.

Ash leaned in closer. "So then what are you here for?" His amber-flecked eyes twinkled beneath his long lashes. "You came to show us Hollywood kids how to have a good party?"

"Not exactly." Jojo felt like she'd break into a million pieces if he didn't kiss her. Right. Now.

She edged ever so slightly closer, so that their knees were touching. A trace of a smile played on Ash's lips, like he thought she might tell him a really juicy secret.

He didn't back away. Jojo saw her chance and leaned in, brushing her lips against his. Every nerve in her candy-coated lips buzzed as she felt Ash's soft lips.

Ash pulled away like he'd been burned.

"What are you doing?" He studied Jojo's face.

She felt heat searing beneath her skin. Embarrassed heat. So hot, she thought her face would surely melt.

Ash looked stricken. He bit his lip thoughtfully, like he was doing long division in his head. Jojo watched as understanding washed over his perfect features. "Oh my God . . . I'm, I—Jojo, I think you're really cool but our whole thing, it was to make Myla jealous. You make an awesome friend but—"

He didn't need to say anything else. He was still in love with Myla. He and Jojo were just the *f*-word. She felt like she was having an out-of-body experience, watching the whole scene play out from above. Ash regarding her with his pitying gaze. Her staring back at him, open-mouthed, her face flushed beyond the alcohol. She was an idiot.

"I better go," Ash said, hopping off the bar stool. He touched Jojo's shoulder and muttered a bland apology before disappearing through the sliding doors to the backyard.

As she spun back to face the bar, the bartender slid another stone sour toward Jojo. "That's rough," he drawled in his laid-back voice. "He's not worth it, though."

Jojo tried to nod, but she was lying to herself and the bartender. Of course Ash was worth it. He was gorgeous. Funny. Sweet. And those eyes. No way would Myla have dated him for three years if he wasn't worthwhile.

She took a sip of her drink, wishing it could make her forget what had just happened. She could feel eyes on her back, but she didn't want to turn around. She decided not to move from her stool until every guest had left, so that she didn't have to make eye contact with anyone who'd just witnessed Ash rejecting her.

"Hey, look up," the hot bartender beckoned. She forced herself to look into his Pacific blue eyes. He leaned across the bar and whispered in her ear. "Don't get hung up on something you can't have. Fuck it, you know? You're not the first person in the world to get blown off by someone who doesn't know a good thing when it's right in front of them."

"I know," Jojo said. And actually . . . he was right. She didn't want her sister's leftovers. She was Barbar's real kid, she was beautiful, and she was getting hotter by the day. She could have someone way better than Ash Gilmour.

"Actually, can you give me something stronger?" She eyed the bartender cockily, daring him to refuse her.

He winked again. "I like your style," he said. "I've got just the thing."

Three Long Island iced teas later, Jojo could barely remember who Ash was, let alone where she was. Tomorrow, she'd tell Willa in full about her evening among Hollywood's finest. She'd had conversations with everyone from Hayden Panettierre to one of the Jonas Brothers, and all of them had been more interested in her than she'd been in them. Being Barbar's daughter meant everyone wanted to suck up to you.

She leaned forward on her stool, slurping down her drink like it was Kool-Aid. The rec room was now over-flowing with people.

Barnsley Toole sidled up, sitting down in the stool next to her. "Feeling good?"

She turned and looked into his face. He had a nice smile, and his eyes seemed friendly. She felt bad for think-ing of him as a flat-faced cat earlier.

"Very much so," Jojo said, feeling cool and confident.

"Must be nice being Barbar's daughter," he continued. "Having all that surplus hotness to throw around."

Jojo swung around on her stool, the movement mak-ing her feel a little seasick. "Yeah, it's working out for me."

Barnsley pushed a curled lock of her hair out from in front of her eyes. "I'll say," he said. "You're the most amazing-looking girl I've seen in a long time."

"Thanks," Jojo demurred, liking the way his fingertips felt against her skin. Who needed Ash?

"I'd like to kiss you," Barnsley said, his other hand lightly brushing her shoulder.

Jojo smiled to herself. This was part of her new life, right? The life of the irresponsible, hard-partying glitterati.

"I'd like that," she answered.

He leaned in, kissing her hard and wet on the mouth. So much saliva, Jojo thought, her stomach lurching. Her mouth tasted sour, and she tried to pull away. Was he this gross or was she about to—

Three Long Islands and two amaretto stone sours burst from Jojo like a ruptured dam.

Barnsley jumped back, a look of disgust and malice all

over his catlike face. "Barbar's daughter just puked in my mouth!" he squealed, spitting on the floor and reaching for a pile of bar napkins. "That fucking bitch just puked in my mouth."

The rec room went silent, as all faces turned to look at Jojo. Her outfit, shoes and bag had miraculously been spared. Barnsley's stool was the major casualty, covered in what were previously cocktails and the In-N-Out burger she'd had for dinner.

Jojo looked around at the shocked, horrified faces of Hollywood's tanned and beautiful best. She felt disgusting. She felt like a loser. She'd spent two years in high school in Sacramento without making this big a fool out of herself.

Barnsley wiped up the mess on his green polo shirt and turned to his camera crew.

"Did you get all that?" he asked, sounding excited now. "That shit is going to kill on YouTube. Barbar? Can you say BarfBarf?"

Jojo, feeling instantly sober, realized that her descent into loserdom wouldn't just be known at BHH, but in Sacramento and the world over. She ran from the rec room to the sound of laughter.

Greenland was looking pretty good right about now.

THIS IS AWKWARD

Amelie was bouncing halfheartedly to Goodbar's cover of the White Stripes' "Seven Nation Army." A small stage had been set up at the far end of the Bufords' three tennis courts, and a few hundred bodies had crammed into the space to see the band play. Goodbar was the latest L.A. band Lewis Buford had taken under his wing, and after appearing on *Gossip Girl*, they were on fire.

Amelie was freezing, but kept resisting Jake's frequent and generous offers of his jacket. The last thing she needed was to finally run into Hunter wearing her math tutor's clothes. Besides, she'd selected her ABS emerald sequin minidress expressly for the skin it tastefully showed off. Covering it up would defeat the purpose.

She and Jake had been through the entire main house, and the two-thousand-square-foot guesthouse, which Lewis had set up as the VIP lounge. They'd also seen most of the hilly grounds where makeshift railings provided support for girls in heels and those too intoxicated to stand up straight. That left the tennis court turned concert hall. But with the throngs of bodies dancing, Amelie could barely see the stage, let alone spot Hunter in the huge crowd.

Jake hadn't left Amelie's side the whole night, and she was grateful not to be entirely alone. As she watched other girls do shots and travel in packs, she felt out of place, like she and Jake were the new kids in school, loners at the shitty lunch table. She half wished she would bump into Kady or anyone else from set. She wished she'd gotten more details from Hunter, so she'd know where to meet him. She'd be disappointed if she spent her whole first date with Hunter just looking for him.

Jake was bobbing his head sort of self-consciously to the music, and Amelie felt a wash of affection for the guy. Maybe once she found Hunter and they were happily hanging out, they could find a girl for Jake.

"Thanks for driving tonight," Amelie said.

Jake smiled goofily, his face surrounded by his unruly curls. "No problem."

She swayed a little more vigorously to the music as the band wound down with a flourish and announced they'd be taking a quick break, before returning with Lewis Buford himself as a guest vocalist.

The crowd instantly thinned, as guys and girls left the tennis court and headed across the yard in pursuit of fresh drinks. What seemed like a hundred guests formed a line in front of the makeshift tiki bar.

"So, um, did you want a drink or anything?"

Amelie shook her head politely. "No thanks, I'm good." Even in her four-inch D&G patent pumps, Amelie still wasn't Jake's height.

Over Jake's shoulder, she caught sight of Hunter's back. Finally! She felt like a little kid on Christmas morning. He'd probably been looking for her all night too. She waited where she stood, hoping he'd turn and see her.

Pushing a lock of red hair from her face, she stared at Hunter's back, chanting in her head, *Turn around. Turn around.* She couldn't wait until he saw her in this dress. She hoped she wasn't turning blue from the cold. Maybe he'd take her someplace quiet inside the house, so they could talk and be alone. Amelie felt jittery as Hunter half turned, revealing his strong chiseled chin and that perfect aquiline nose. But then Amelie saw who he was talking to: a pretty brunette, in a dress that revealed more limbs than the magnolia trees in Lewis's backyard.

They were talking and laughing, the brunette's hand on Hunter's arm. But that was no big deal, right? Amelie was here with Jake, and that was purely a friends thing. *Or*, Amelie thought, mildly ashamed, *a using-your-friends thing.*

She took a few tentative steps toward Hunter. She could cut in and introduce herself to his friend. She had nothing to be nervous about. Hunter had asked *her* here, to be his date to the party.

She clacked across the tennis court, nearing Hunter just as he leaned down and planted a long, deep kiss on the brunette's lips. Amelie stopped dead in her tracks.

Her knees buckled. She felt like the tennis court was going to crumble out from underneath her.

And then it hit her: She'd set herself up for this very disappointment. If this had been a date, wouldn't Hunter have picked her up? Or made sure she knew where to meet him? Or asked for her *phone number*? Amelie felt her face flush red with embarrassment, disappointment, and rejection.

So they'd hung out at Area. He'd given her a kiss on the cheek, even after she'd sent multiple signals that he could have gone for a full-on kiss—like the one he continued to share with the brunette. Hunter didn't have feelings for her. He was friendly, professional, and about as flirty as she'd been with poor Jake.

Feeling tears prick at the corner of her eyes, Amelie did a three-sixty from the sight of Hunter and the girl. She fled in the direction of a terrace along the side of the mansion.

Jake watched Amelie run off. *Oh my God,* he thought. *What did I do?* He cursed himself and his un-smooth ways. He should have asked her to dance. Or maybe she'd wanted him to take her somewhere to talk. He'd taken her out to hear the band play, because he'd thought the crowded tennis court was the most low-pressure spot he could choose. But clearly, Amelie was not having a good time.

He followed her to the terrace, feeling determined. He would tell Amelie that he liked her and that he hadn't meant to be so quiet. He tried to muster as much manliness as he could, given that his *Battlestar Galactica*–obsessed friend had dressed him tonight.

The terrace was nearly empty, save for a couple making out behind a potted palm in one corner. Amelie stood in the other corner, staring into space as she leaned over the railing. The corners of her turquoise eyes were wet.

Jake hopped up the terrace's small, shallow steps and quietly approached Amelie.

"Hey," he murmured. Just do this, he told himself. Tell her not to cry. Tell her she's amazing. *Tell her you like her.*

He could feel the words at the top of his throat, ready to float their way to Amelie's ears. He pictured her sad expression replaced by a happy one as each word reached her. She'd lift her chin, her eyelids widening from their half-mast state. A smile would turn her lips up in a curve of pleasure. He took her hand, producing a cocktail napkin from his pocket.

Amelie took the napkin with a weak smile and turned to him. She was staring at him . . . expectantly? Curiously? He wasn't really sure. Jake cleared his throat. He wasn't going to make the first romantic overture of his life with a cracking voice.

The door from the house to the terrace swung open behind him with a creak. So what if someone else was here? Let them listen. He was crazy about this girl and had nothing to hide.

"Don't cry," he began, pausing when he saw that Amelie was no longer looking at him. She peered over his shoulder, her tiny hand still loosely gripping his.

A hint of a smile, or something like relief, took over the rest of her face.

"Hunter," she said.

Jake turned to look behind him. Awesome. Hunter "Hottest Under 25" Sparks had joined them on the terrace. He might as well have ridden up on a majestic steed or something, he looked so heroic in his plain green T-shirt under a gray military-style jacket and jeans. Were those regular old Levi's? Jake felt like an idiot with his artfully frayed back pockets.

Hunter stepped toward Amelie, ignoring Jake as though he were just one of the terrace's weatherproof ottomans.

"Are you okay?" Hunter asked, placing a hand on Amelie's bare shoulder. "I saw you run off from the tennis courts." He still hadn't acknowledged Jake. "Why don't I take you home?"

Amelie nodded. Without ceremony, she dropped Jake's hand.

"See you on Monday, okay, Jake?" Amelie turned to face him, her eyes glimmering a darker blue with the remainder of her tears.

Jake fought his urge to yell, *But I like you. I'd do anything for you. Don't go with him!* Instead, he uttered an "Okay."

Hunter took off his jacket, draped it over Amelie's shoulders, and—his arm around her waist—steered her from the terrace with only a curt nod to Jake. Like Jake had been the one taking Amelie away from him.

The couple making out on the terrace paused, taking in the show. Jake heard the guy murmur, "Was that Amelie Adams with Hunter Sparks?"

Jake deflated. Of course it was. How had he been stupid enough to believe this was a date? Amelie had used him to get to the party, and he'd fallen under her spell as easily as if she'd enchanted him with her Fairy Princess wand.

Things really *had* changed for Jake this school year. They'd gotten much, much worse.

DEADLY KISS

Ash sat alone on a Mod Abode teak sun lounger, guzzling a Stella as he looked blankly across the empty, still pool. It was past midnight, and he still hadn't found Myla. A few seats away, his friend Tucker groped a UCLA coed whose long dirty blond waves disturbingly reminded Ash of his sister, Tessa. The girl kept running her hand over Tucker's recently shaved Downy-soft head.

The Goodbar performance was in full swing, and Ash could see the stage clearly from where he sat. Lewis Buford was guest singing for Goodbar. He strutted around the stage cockily, holding the mike between two hands, every so often pumping his fist like a demented, sweaty Bono.

"My name is Lewis Buford, and I'm a rockaholic."

Ash scoffed, rolling his eyes at a group of girls in front of the stage in matching halter tops mooning up at Lewis. The whole tennis court was filled with writhing bodies, eager to catch Lewis's performance. How they could dance to Lewis's off-pitch vocals was beyond Ash.

He took another swig of beer, wishing Myla would

materialize next to him. Since he'd gotten her invitation yesterday, he'd been resisting the urge to just call her—she'd accused him of being needy, and he wanted to show her that he could survive without her for a day. He'd already done it for five. He'd looked for her in the house and on the tennis courts with no luck. He really didn't want to circle the party again. He feared bumping into Jojo, whom he'd left dejected and angry an hour before. He really felt crappy about the situation. Why couldn't you hang with your ex's new sister to make your ex jealous without it getting all emotional?

And how had things gotten so complicated?

Myla would probably know where he'd gone wrong. Once they'd happily gotten back together, he'd tell her to treat Jojo a little better. Maybe they could hang out, the three of them. Tucker thought Jojo was totally cute, so maybe he could do a little matchmaking or something. Myla was good at that stuff, when she was feeling generous.

Squinting across the water, Ash rescanned the crowd. Even with the prospect of running into an angry Jojo, he knew he'd eventually have to continue roaming the party in search of Myla. Unless she wasn't here?

He slowly swallowed a fresh gulp of the cold beer. That was a possibility he refused to consider.

Myla involuntarily played with the gold chain that once had held her Green Lantern ring. She'd replaced the ring with a delicate hummingbird charm of no particular significance, except that it didn't remind her of Ash. But she still couldn't break the habit of touching the chain.

Instead of going the minidress-up-to-there-with-heels route, which was becoming de rigueur at these events, Myla had worn her dark denim Rock & Republic jeans that made her butt look amazing with a simple American Apparel cami in royal blue. She topped it off with a fitted gray hoodie that was actually Mahalo's and wore her slightly weathered Frye boots. Her hair tumbled over her shoulders in a way that looked effortless but had taken hours. For makeup, she'd opted for her creamy Stila highlighter with a touch of shimmer, and golden eye shadow that made her green eyes pop. Glamour didn't have to mean excess glitz. *Try telling that to Fortune Weathers*, Myla thought. Her friend's Swarovski crystal–encrusted shift dress looked like it weighed about two thousand pounds, and made her walk like a caveman.

Myla was standing next to a makeshift tiki bar alongside the tennis court, tapping her boot soundlessly against the verdant, high-maintenance lawn. She was waiting on her third Grey Goose and tonic as she watched Lewis Buford perform, while hoping to catch Ash in her peripheral vision.

The last time she'd been here, almost two years ago, Ash and Lewis had been working on a new song together with Myla as their muse. She remembered how they'd gone from rhyming words with "dark" to arguing about who would be the lead singer. Ash had stormed out and Myla had followed. She'd left behind her new Vince bomber jacket and had returned to the house to get it. Lewis had backed her into a corner of his foyer, trying to kiss her, telling her he was better than Ash in every way. Ash had rescued her in the nick of time, charging through the door, punching Lewis in the jaw, and leading Myla to safety. It was one of Myla's best memories, not least of all because that day was the first time Ash told her he loved her.

"Thank you, and good morning, bitches!" Lewis was wrapping up the band's set with a flourish, raising his arms in the air to command more applause for his performance. His face in a satisfied rock-god grin, he leapt off the stage and made a beeline for Myla.

He beamed at her, his whitened teeth bordering on glow-in-the-dark. She couldn't have paid Lewis to look this happy to see her.

Myla loved when she had a plan. Even better was when everything started to fall into place. After she'd sent Ash the invite to Lewis's party yesterday, she'd called Lewis and engaged him in some flirty banter. When she mentioned his party, she could practically hear him salivating at the prospect of having her in his house. He'd had a thing for her for ages.

Lewis had told her to come see his set with Goodbar, starting at midnight. Now all she had to do was flirt like crazy in Ash's sight line, and he'd know exactly how she'd felt the other day in Jojo's room. These days, "an eye for an eye" was practically Myla's mantra.

Lewis grabbed her by the arm, his grip uncomfortably tight. "Hey, hotness," he said, leading her away from the crowd. "Let's hit VIP. Did you hear some chick barfed on Barnsley? I have *got* to get that story."

Myla smiled, picturing that loser Barnsley getting puked on. Lewis led her behind the stage toward the guesthouse. "You were great onstage," she lied.

"I know," Lewis said, turning back to grin at her as he pushed through the door of the guesthouse. Myla smirked to herself. Ash would definitely know to look for her here. Beyond it being where they used to hang out when Ash and Lewis were friends, Ash knew she'd always choose the most exclusive section of any social event. "I can't wait till I get my own band together again. You'll come to all our shows, right?"

She tossed her long hair over her shoulder, giving Lewis her sexiest stare. "Hell, yeah," she said. "I can't wait." Flirting with Lewis should technically have been easy, because he was ridiculously good looking. His thick, dark hair was always slightly mussed, and he had a dimple in his left cheek. But he was so full of himself. Tonight, he wore a shirt screen-printed with his baby photo: Lewis on a bearskin rug, naked.

Lewis grinned wolfishly, pulling her into the guesthouse's living room, which had an airy, beach house feel to it. The living area was one big room strewn with artfully rumpled sofas and love seats in off-white linen surrounding a low white coffee table. An oversize photo of the Santa Cruz boardwalk—an amusement park in Northern California made famous in *The Lost Boys*—took up half of one aqua blue wall.

The low thrum of the Strokes' new album issued from an iPod in the corner. Myla glanced around, looking for Ash. He wasn't here, but Geoff was—with Billie sprawled comfortably in his lap. If Geoff was here, Tucker would follow, and eventually so would Ash. Ash and his boys were lost without one another. Perfect.

Lewis lifted a bottle of chilled Veuve from an ice bucket

near the door. "I propose a toast," he purred, grabbing two champagne flutes from a faux-weathered armoire.

Myla nodded. She was feeling pretty celebratory herself. Lewis poured some Veuve into the flutes, and she plucked one from his hand.

He leaned in so that their faces were inches apart. "I'm so glad you ditched that loser, Gilmour."

Myla took a sip of Veuve, enjoying the bubbles as they fizzed down her throat.

"Me too." She flashed Lewis her irresistible half smile. Now if only that loser Gilmour would actually show up.

"So, did you just fall from heaven, angel?"

Ash sauntered past the pool, winding around that prick Barnsley Toole, who, Ash noticed, was on his second outfit of the night. He was throwing choice pickup lines at a girl who looked like she'd just stepped off a bus from the Land of Gullibility.

Ash wandered first in the direction of the main house, but, remembering Jojo's pissed expression, stopped when he saw Tucker walking toward the guesthouse. Or VIP lounge, as that idiot Buford was calling it.

The guesthouse's door was wide open, and Ash laughed to himself. Some exclusive VIP experience. Still, Myla couldn't resist a VIP anything. Ash hoped she was inside, waiting for him.

The main room was nearly empty, with a few couples sprawled on couches. Ash saw his friend Geoff rubbing Billie Bollman's feet, a pickup move Geoff reinstated every time he watched *Pulp Fiction.*

"Geoff, you see Myla?" Ash asked urgently.

Geoff looked up over Billie's maroon-painted toe-nails. "Um, yeah, I saw her," his friend drawled slowly. He was too drunk or stoned to be of any use. Ash waved off Geoff's response and made his way down the hall-way.

He headed toward the greenroom, which had been his and Lewis's favorite spot back when they were friends. Instead of carpet, the green-room floor was covered in thick green grass that felt real. Lewis's dad, a former player for the Oakland A's who now ran a consultancy firm for teams building and upgrading their stadiums, had used the material on a soccer stadium in Chicago. His mem-ory flashed to the day Lewis's father had ordered the turf for this room. Mr. Buford had instructed Lewis and Ash to pick out the furniture, and Ash had come up with a bunch of mondo-size orange felt LoveSacs. Lewis's dad had loved the idea, and Ash remembered how proud he felt to have an adult's acknowledgment for a change.

Ash froze as he approached the green room's door-way. Now, on one of those very beanbags, sat Myla, a champagne flute dangling from her fingers, leaning back alongside Lewis.

Myla shifted on the oversize beanbag, leaning against Lewis's muscular chest and laughing at the bad joke she hadn't been paying attention to.

"You are so hot," Lewis said, for about the fiftieth time that night. Yawn. He was looking down at her with dark blue eyes that bore not a hint of brain activity behind them.

"You're not so bad yourself," Myla said robotically. Suddenly she became aware of the fact that Ash was standing in the doorway. Her whole body tensed, and she tried to focus all her attention on Lewis, even though her eyes wanted to lock gazes with Ash.

Lewis breathed hot on her cheek, and before Myla knew what was happening, his lips were on hers. He used so much force and speed, it felt like he had two tongues.

Lewis ran a rough hand through her hair. *Take that, Ash,* Myla thought, and kissed Lewis right back. She hadn't planned to take it this far, but she couldn't plan everything out, now could she?

Ash felt like someone had pushed pause on his life. And now, he was just stalled in this doorway, frozen in the worst scene of all his seventeen years.

Myla, his Myla. Her thick glossy hair spilled over Lewis Buford's fingertips. Her long, lean thighs rested over Lewis's legs. Her lithe waist clutched tightly by Lewis's meaty paw. Her dark red lips locked in a deep kiss. A kiss administered by Ash's worst enemy. Ash gagged, tasting stale Stella.

While Myla was away, he'd had nightmares like this. In them, Myla was always hand in hand with some random guy she'd supposedly met in Africa or Asia or somewhere. She'd show up at Ash's door and kiss the guy in front of him. He always woke up with a start right after the part where Myla turned her half smile on him and casually said, "We're done."

But at least in those dreams, it was always some Peace Corps dude Ash didn't know. This was way, way worse. Lewis Buford had squelched Ash's musical career. He'd stolen his best song, too. He'd tried before to make a play for Myla. Now it was Lewis who sang onstage. Lewis who'd stolen Deadly Kiss as his record label name. And Lewis happily entwined with Myla.

He didn't know if he wanted to pull Lewis up by his collar and punch him, or lift Myla up and carry her away, or reverse the fact he'd ever been born.

Finally, finally, Lewis Buford's grip on the back of Myla's head loosened. She pulled away, faking a dreamy look. She wanted Ash to think Lewis was the best kisser ever.

She casually leaned back on the beanbag, her eyes landing on Ash. He'd taken a few steps into the room, and loomed over her and Lewis. His chestnut eyes glinted down at her with anger and disgust.

Myla felt her face draw itself into a mask of tension. Her heart started to beat in double time. She forced herself to breathe, even though an air bubble lodged itself between her throat and her chest.

Where was the satisfaction? She was supposed to feel victorious. She'd had the last laugh. Right?

Yet she felt like crying. Shame coursed through her body as Ash wordlessly regarded her, his eyelids lowered as he looked at her like she'd just crushed his favorite guitar.

"So this is why you invited me?" Ash finally spoke. "Just part of your plan?"

Suddenly cold, Myla pulled her hoodie tight around her, sitting up as straight as she could in the LoveSac. "No. I mean, I don't know." She felt queasy, but not from the vodka and champagne mingling in her stomach. Her stomach felt like it was plunging over and over again, like she was on a roller coaster that only went down.

Lewis lazily threw his arm over Myla's shoulder, kneading her arm. "She came for me, Gilmour."

Ash didn't look at him. His eyes never left Myla as he backed away like she was a rattlesnake in the grass at Griffith Park.

Myla had never seen Ash's face so still. Usually his eyes at least twinkled with a random thought or a joke or some mischievous idea he'd had. Right now, he looked like a replica of Ash Gilmour, stored behind glass and immobile. Myla shivered, feeling alone and hopeless. This was low. Even for her. She might as well be on an ice block in the middle of the ocean, instead of this beanbag chair. She reached for her gold chain. It was broken. It dangled, open on one end, from her neck.

Ash watched her fumble with the chain, his face still a blank mask. He turned on his heels without a word to her. "Go to hell, Buford," was all he said as he stalked off.

Myla felt like she was already there.

NUUK, NUUK, WHO'S THERE?

"It's okay, Jojo," Fred's voice soothed, static crackling over the line. "Worse things have happened."

"Not to me," Jojo mumbled, running the toe of her shoe over the gravel in the driveway. "I really screwed up." She paced near the end of the circular driveway, waiting for the Everharts' town car to show up. The air was cool and dry up in the Hollywood Hills, and Jojo wished she'd brought a sweater.

After calling for the car, Jojo had called her dads. She was ready to end her life in Hollywood and escape to Nuuk. She'd told them everything. Well, almost everything. She'd edited her five drinks down to one and told them she'd puked on Barnsley Toole, but not that she'd been making out with him when it happened. "You didn't screw up. I mean, I speak for both of us when I say that we're disappointed you were drinking but maybe you learned something about your limits," Bradley soothed. "We don't want you to regret leaving so quickly. Lailah and Barkley love having you. Maybe you should sleep on it."

Jojo heaved a deep sigh. She wouldn't sleep tonight.

She'd pack. And tomorrow, she'd take the first flight out of Beverly Hills.

"I'll do that," she lied, anxious to be with her dads again, far away from the remnants of her briefly fabulous life. Really she was going to head home, grab her things, say goodbye, and head straight for LAX. "I promise. I love you guys."

"We love you too," Fred and Barkley uttered simultaneously.

Jojo hung up, wishing she'd turned down Myla's invitation to come to the party tonight. Why couldn't she have taken things more slowly? What had made her think she could be plucked from steady-as-she-goes Sacramento and land on her feet in the Hollywood high life? She'd been such a fool, thinking it was so easy to be Little Miss Fabulous just because of her famous parents. She should have tested the waters a little. Instead, she'd jumped in and drowned.

Now sober, Jojo realized her feet were killing her. She headed to the center of the lawn, where she'd seen a white gazebo covered in bougainvillea flowers that grew through the latticework. She plopped down on a wicker chair inside the gazebo, her eyes on the long driveway. The front yard was quiet, everyone still in the house or out back, listening to the band play. Unbuckling her left shoe, she heard crying coming from the other side of bougainvillea.

Shoe in hand, Jojo tottered on one wedge and one bare foot across the lawn. On a long stone bench just outside the gazebo, Myla had her knees pulled up and her head down, a ball of thick long hair and expensive denim.

Jojo tapped Myla on the shoulder, the hem of her dress touching Myla's boots.

Myla looked up, her eyes glistening with fresh tears as old ones made their way down her cheeks. Leave it to her to be a blubbering mess and still look beautiful. Jojo knew her own eye makeup was smeared across her cheek and her hair was a mass of tangles.

"What are you doing here?" Myla asked, slowly unfolding herself. Her legs dangled off the edge of the bench.

"Waiting on my ride." Jojo bent, unbuckling her other shoe. "You can stop crying. I'm leaving. For good. You can have Mom and Dad all to yourself again."

Myla furrowed her brow, pulling her sweatshirt tight around her. She scanned Jojo from head to toe with wide, honest eyes, as though examining her for damage. It was the first time Myla had looked at Jojo without malice, jealousy, disgust, or fake sisterly love.

"I'm not crying over you," Myla said, like it was the most ridiculous thing in the world. "I'm crying over Ash." She shifted away, leaving Jojo staring dumbly down at a bright pink bougainvillea blossom.

"Ash?" *Join the club*, Jojo thought, an image of Ash rejecting her replaying in her head. Even when she was a billion miles away, going to Viking school in Nuuk, Jojo knew she'd remember Ash. Hanging out with him had made her feel like anything was possible in L.A.

"I really don't want to talk about it with you." Myla's voice sounded little in the darkness, and for the first time ever, Jojo felt sorry for her.

She sat down on the bench softly. "Fine," she sighed,

playing with the straps of her shoes as they dangled from her hand. "But the day you saw us hanging out? That was just to get to you." Jojo wasn't sure what made her admit it, but seeing Myla like this made her feel guilty holding it in.

Myla twisted on the bench. She looked at Jojo questioningly.

"He wouldn't go to all that trouble to make you jealous if he didn't still care about you," Jojo said simply, wishing she'd understood that an hour ago, before she'd made a mess of her life. As much as it hurt to say it, it was the truth.

A fresh sob escaped from Myla's throat.

"But he came here so we could make up. And then he saw me kissing Lewis Buford," Myla heaved. "His archnemesis."

Jojo chuckled. "That guy? Isn't he wearing his own face on his shirt?"

Myla laughed. The tinkling, joyful sound made Jojo feel good, knowing she'd caused it. "I know. What was I thinking? He's so gross. And now there's no going back to Ash."

Jojo lightly touched Myla's arm. "He'll get over it."

Myla didn't flinch from Jojo's hand, and Jojo smiled faintly. It felt weird, sharing this close moment with a girl who'd made her life hell this past week. *Maybe if we hadn't been sisters, we could have been friends,* Jojo thought.

Myla finally smiled, a little devilishly. "Speaking of finding giant assholes to kiss, I hear you hurled on Barnsley Toole."

Jojo winced at the memory, just as Charlie pulled the

dark town car into the driveway. Word had gotten around fast.

"Yeah, I did." Jojo nodded, standing up from the bench. The velvety grass tickled her bare feet. She headed toward the car, giving Myla a half wave as she climbed into the backseat. She gazed at the illuminated stucco of Lewis Buford's mansion, saying goodbye to it in her head. Goodbye to Beverly Hills. Goodbye to Fred Segal. Goodbye to Lailah and Barkley.

As Charlie came around to close her door, Myla noticed Jojo's Rittenhouse bag still on the bench.

She grabbed it, jogged to the car, and thrust it through the open door at Jojo. "Puking on that piece of crap Barnsley is the first thing you've done that I agree with. Besides picking out this bag, anyway."

Jojo smiled wanly. "Keep it. It's not my style."

Myla shrugged, pulling the bag neatly over her arm. "See you, Jojo."

"Goodbye, Myla."

The door closed.

HEARTBREAKER

Amelie sat in the passenger seat of Hunter's Prius, eyeing the front of her house. She hoped her mom was asleep and she could slip in wearing her sequined dress. The backpack containing her "tutoring" outfit was still in Jake's Corolla.

The drive from the Hollywood Hills to Toluca Lake had only taken about fifteen minutes, and she and Hunter hadn't said much the whole ride. Amelie had tried to imagine they were going on a weekend trip to Big Sur up the PCH. But every time she pictured him unlocking the door to their cabin, she saw him with the brunette from the party instead of with herself.

A short-haired woman in yoga pants and a Chanel suit jacket crossed Navajo, being led by three Labradoodles. Amelie watched her pass under a street lamp and disappear. Hunter turned off the headlights. He rubbed his short hair, his head cocked to one side, facing her. "So what happened back there?" He scanned her face. "Did that guy break your heart or something?"

It took Amelie a second to determine that Hunter

wasn't talking in the third person. He was asking about Jake. He thought *Jake* had broken her heart.

Amelie knew she could set him straight right then and there. She could tell Hunter that she liked *him*. That she wanted desperately for him to see her as more than a friend, a coworker, a little girl, whatever it was that was blocking him from seeing her as a girl his age who wanted nothing more than to go on one date with him, just to see what could happen. But fear pushed the words back into her throat. If she told Hunter her true feelings, it could be a disaster. She had to see him on set and couldn't bear for things to become awkward between them.

"Yeah, he did," Amelie lied. He'd given her the perfect way out.

Hunter sighed deeply, shaking his head. "Let me walk you up."

He got out on his side and jogged around to open her door. He steered her to the front door with his hand on the small of her back.

Only the porch light was on, so Helen must have been asleep. Amelie sighed inwardly. At least she wouldn't have to deal with an interrogation tonight. She certainly hadn't done anything wrong, except think Hunter's party invitation was a date. She pulled her key from her sparkly clutch.

Hunter touched her shoulder, turning her around to face him. Standing beneath the porch's spotlight, he looked like the ultimate romantic hero. He searched Amelie's face intently. The moment was just like she'd imagined it, except in her daydreams, Hunter wasn't consoling her over a crush gone wrong.

"You know that I'll always be here for you," he said, staring at her seriously. "You're like my little sister."

That's exactly the problem, Amelie thought.

"Thanks, Hunter," she said, turning her key over in her hand.

"I mean it, Amelie," he said, a sad look on his face. "You need someone like me to look out for you. Because, honestly, there are a lot of guys out there—guys like me, who can't resist you. And you're too good for us." With that, he leaned down and kissed her lightly on the cheek. He hopped down the steps, leaving Amelie standing on the porch.

She watched him pull away from the curb, feeling a fresh glimmer of hope. *Guys like me, who can't resist you.*

She could deal with that. At least for now.

MISERY LOVES EGGS BENEDICT

"Jacob, you haven't touched your pancakes." Jake's mom Gigi eyed his stack of buttermilk pancakes with envy as she took another bite of her breakfast salad. One of her clients was having a beach wedding in a few weeks, and Gigi was trying the veggie cleanse that Demi had gushed about on Oprah the month before.

Gigi and Jonathan sat across from Jake, watching every bite he *wasn't* taking. Next to him, his little brother, Brendan, plowed through his second stack of pancakes.

Jake was slumped in a booth at Hugo's in West Hollywood, possibly the most popular brunch spot in the world. If you read the little history on the menu—which Jake had done on a dozen different visits as his parents lingered over one last cappuccino—Hugo's credited itself with starting Hollywood's power breakfast trend in the 1980s, when Spielberg, Lucas, and John Landis met to do business over breakfast. Now, it was *the* place for Sunday brunch. As usual, every table in the place was packed, the chatter of other diners drowning out Jake's thoughts. In the booth next to them, Scott Caan read the *L.A. Times* over his Pasta Mama. Across the crowded dining room,

Sarah Michelle Gellar and Freddie Prinze Jr. gave their orders to a tall, skinny waiter, whose artfully gelled hair suggested he had a stack of head shots in his trunk.

Jake didn't understand why his mom thought he could eat at a time like this. He'd told his family the whole sad story. That he'd thought Amelie—Amelie "Beautiful Starlet Worth Millions" Adams—liked him. That he'd read maybe one thousand web pages in an effort to learn everything about her. That he'd dropped pretty much all his summer camp earnings buying overpriced jeans that Amelie wouldn't have noticed unless they caught fire. That he hadn't guessed she was using him to take her to Lewis Buford's party until Hunter Sparks had shown up. That he was going to feel like an idiot the next time he went to her trailer for tutoring in his pathetic Corolla. That he'd left Lewis's party alone, feeling like every guest knew he'd been rejected. Even Miles hadn't been able to console him with a deluded pep talk. His only response had been, "That's rough, Jake, really rough."

Gigi sighed, relenting as she stabbed a pancake with her fork and made room for it on her plate. Cutting it carefully, she closed her eyes and took a bite. Jonathan, with his oversize bowl of Pasta Papa—a pasta dish made breakfast-friendly with eggs and sausage mixed in—laughed with affection at his wife. Gigi reached across the table, putting her hand over Jake's.

"Do you know how many people I see make colossal mistakes every day?" Her wide brown eyes surveyed Jake's hangdog face. "And people forget—they always forget. Nothing is ever as bad as it seems."

"Except for thinking you can nail Fairy Princess,"

Brendan piped up through a mouthful of pancake. "Moron."

Gigi slapped Brendan's hand. "Language! And how many times do I have to ask you to take off that fucking hat?" Gigi had a tough time enforcing a no-swearing rule with her boys when she was the household's worst offender.

Brendan rolled his eyes, removing his Dodgers cap and shaking out his light brown curls. "Focus on Jake, mom, and his delusions of scoring hot chicks."

Jake poked his brother hard in the ribs. Brendan looked toward his parents to scold his older sibling, but they turned a blind eye. They felt sorry for Jake. Which just made him feel worse.

"Are you paying attention to me, Jacob?" Gigi speared another bite of pancake as Jonathan let loose a chuckle loud enough to make Sarah Michelle look their way.

He nodded halfheartedly, avoiding eye contact as he twirled a parsley sprig between his thumb and forefinger.

Swallowing a sip of his coffee, Jonathan cleared his throat. He patted his wide belly and leaned across the table so he was closer to his son.

"Maybe you should start with a lady-in-waiting, instead of the princess herself," he half whispered. His dad chuckled at his own dumb joke and his mom slapped him playfully on the shoulder.

Jake sighed. "Don't worry about it guys, it's no big deal."

His mom shook her head, as if to say, *You idiot.*

"You're our son, Jacob," she said, popping another sliver of pancake into her mouth. "Of course it's a big deal."

Jonathan put his arm around Gigi. "Son, I didn't land your mother until I'd dated a dozen women who weren't even half her equal. Brainy types like us have to start small. You don't learn to mountain climb by heading straight for Everest." Brendan rolled his eyes, grossed out by the parental affection.

Gigi snuggled into Jonathan's shoulder. "And you're not always going to be driving a Corolla, Jake. Things get better after high school."

"You mean if he changes his identity and stuff, right?" Brendan gurgled through a swig of orange juice. "Spell out all the conditions, guys."

Jonathan scowled at his younger son. His features softened and he looked Jacob in the eye. "Trust us, Jake."

Jake broke the parsley sprig between his fingers. He knew he was lucky to have parents who'd work so hard to try to cheer him up. But all the parental support in the world wasn't going to heal his broken heart.

THE LAST WALTZ

Ash played with his iPhone's touch screen, pressing Myla Everhart in his contacts list. A photo he'd taken of her at Manhattan Beach came up next to her number. She was blowing a kiss at him, her face half shaded by the wide, white sun hat she wore.

He lay on his bed, a copy of *Guitar* magazine open on his chest. He'd had trouble falling asleep after the party last night. He'd kept closing his eyes to see Myla with Lewis, locked at the lips. At 3 a.m., he'd given up on sleep and tinkered with his guitar for a few hours. Finally, he'd drifted off into dreamless sleep. When he woke at noon, he felt purposeful, like he knew what he had to do.

He pressed the call button. Myla's phone rang three times, then four. On the fifth ring, she picked up. Her voice sounded hazy and tired.

"Can you meet me at our place?" Ash asked shortly.

"Yeah, of course." She sounded confused.

"Okay, see you at three." Ash hung up. They'd talk later.

For once, Ash was early. He plopped down in the shade of a knotty, gigantic tree and watched the Griffith

Park carousel as it spun a little too fast, playing a tinny waltz that was barely audible over the kids' shrieks and giggles. Parents clicked away on cameras or stared in terror as their babies clung to the old wooden horses.

This spot of the park was his and Myla's place. Two years ago, Ash had taken her here for a picnic on her birthday. He'd called Canter's Deli and ordered a massive spread—miniature sandwiches, sparkling grape juice, homemade potato chips, and chocolate cake. He'd even snuck a bottle of Dom from his dad's wine cellar—the first time he'd ever stolen from his parents' alcohol stash. It was a school day but they'd ditched, and the park had been nearly empty except for them. On the way there, they'd stopped at a grocery store in Silver Lake because Ash had forgotten cups. They'd bought surprises for each other from the store's '50s bubble gum machine and traded them while toasting with Solo cups of Dom. He'd given her a Green Lantern plastic band and she'd presented him with a flimsy pseudo-gold lightning bolt. They'd been wearing each other's rings since then.

Even though it butted right up to the Golden State Freeway, Griffith Park made you feel like you weren't in L.A. anymore. You couldn't hear any of the traffic or noise of the city, and the park felt slightly wild and untamed in places, so you could almost imagine what the rest of L.A. had been like before it became populated with freeways, movie studios, and shopping malls.

The last time they'd been here was right before Myla left on her trip. She and Ash wanted to get away from their families and friends. They'd come to the park to look for the L.A. zoo's old animal cages, which now sat next to a picnic area. Myla had even tried hiking, making it about twenty feet up a dirt path in her kitten heels. Ash had had to carry her back down. Then he'd paid the carousel operators to let them ride it by themselves for three songs in a row. They'd shared a horse, which Myla named Sparky, and giggled crazily through the whole ride. They got off, giddy and dizzy, before collapsing next to each other in the grass under the tree where Ash was sitting now.

He closed his eyes and leaned back against the tree's rough bark, running his finger over a small hole near the bottom of the Rolling Stones T-shirt he held in his lap.

"Hi Ash." Myla's voice tinkled in his ear. He opened one eyelid and gazed up at her. She looked angelic. Rays of sunlight lit her from behind, and the emerald hoop earrings she wore sparkled around her face. Her huge white Gucci sunglasses were perched on her head, and Ash found himself staring at her glittering green eyes underneath the fringe of her long eyelashes. The sounds of the carousel and the kids faded, and all Ash could hear was his heart beating and Myla's breathing. If he could create the most beautiful girl in the world, he'd end up with one that looked just like Myla right now, with her dark pink lips in their familiar half smile.

"Hi Myla," he finally managed. He didn't know what he wanted—not exactly. As much as he wanted to pull her close and feel her soft cheek against his neck, the image of Myla entwined with Lewis rushed into his head, overtaking everything. Calling up every ounce of strength and willpower he had, he launched into the speech he'd been mulling since that morning.

"Okay, I just wanted to finally clear the air," Ash began. "We've both been acting like jerks because we're broken up, and we're so used to being together. But we have to act like human beings. We see each other all the time; we have a lot of the same friends. We've been a couple since we were kids, so maybe it's hard to be mature. But we need to be." He thrust the balled-up Stones shirt at Myla. "I thought you should have this back," he said. "It looks better on you anyway."

Myla tentatively took the shirt. The worn, familiar cotton felt foreign in her hands. This hadn't been what she was expecting at all. She knew Ash was mad after what happened last night, but she'd really thought he'd asked her here to get back together. That seeing her with Lewis had pushed him over the edge and he needed to know she was still his girl.

The ground beneath Myla's ivory Lanvin flats felt like it was pulling her down. She and Ash were really done. Truly over. He didn't seem mad at her at all, which actually made her feel worse. Like his feelings had evaporated overnight.

Myla pretended to squint into the sun, so she'd have an excuse to pull her sunglasses down over her eyes. She tucked the T-shirt into the Martin Rittenhouse bag Jojo had given her. The shirt was no longer part of their future together. It had become nothing more than an artifact of something long gone.

Finally, she nodded, nervously smoothing her white silk BCBG empire-waist sundress. "Thanks," she said, her voice as even as her recently filed fingernails. "I've always liked this shirt." She turned to head to the waiting SUV, biting her lip to keep it from trembling.

"Hey Myla?" Ash was still standing under their tree, the hint of a smile on his lips.

She turned back, praying her face didn't look like a telethon orphan's. "Yeah?"

"Remember that night? How you did your whole badass act with the bouncer, and told him your parents were Barkley Everhart and Lailah Barton and if they didn't let us backstage, you could have the Avalon shut down?" Ash's eyes were dancing with laughter.

"Oh yeah, I wanted to impress you. But we really got back there because your dad had the whole concert set up just for our date. And you didn't have the heart to tell me, even though I'd already called my parents and their agents were calling the band's people to get us back there." Myla couldn't help but laugh too, remembering.

Ash shrugged, watching as a guy jogged by with four Great Danes. "Well, you were so proud of yourself. And I thought it was so cool a girl would threaten the Stones' security guards just for me."

"I barely knew who the band even was." Myla ran the flat sole of her gladiator sandal over the dry ground. "I remember telling the guard, 'Rick and Heath will have to personally answer to my parents.'"

Ash widened his eyes, incredulous. "You seriously called Mick Jagger and Keith Richards *Rick and Heath*? Wow. I'll have to burn you a few CDs soon. You need an education."

Myla rolled her eyes. "Come on, who was it that took you to see the Arctic Monkeys before you'd even heard of them?" She'd been so pleased, discovering the band before Ash did in a copy of *Q* her dad had brought back from a trip to London. She'd taken Ash to the band's first U.S. show at the Wiltern for his birthday.

Ash shrugged, his sandy hair falling in front of his sleepy puppy-dog eyes. "Yeah, okay. But I'll bring you a few CDs anyway. It can't hurt."

Myla grinned, pulling her sunglasses back to the top of her head. She giggled as a half-dozen little kids ran past, red helium balloons tied to their chubby wrists. "No, probably not."

Ash nodded, satisfied. "Cool. So, I guess I'll . . . see you?"

Myla smiled, not exactly sure how she felt but knowing she wasn't going to cry. "Yeah, see you."

She took a few steps backwards, waving to Ash as she went. He didn't take his eyes off her. Suddenly, even her fingertips felt tingly.

She finally turned away from Ash, the park's brush-covered ground springy under her feet. When she knew he couldn't see her any longer, she reached in her purse, running her fingertips along the shirt's soft, brushed cotton.

Softly she sang the opening verse of her favorite Stones song, "Happy." She'd memorized the lyrics after listening to it about a hundred times on the beach with Ash.

Well I never kept a dollar past sunset. / It always burned a hole in my pants. / Never made a school mama happy. / Never blew a second chance, oh no.

Never blew a second chance, oh no, indeed.

HOLLYWOOD ENDING

Jojo watched as David, the Everharts' backup driver, loaded her overstuffed Samsonite suitcase into the town car's vast trunk. She felt bad that she wouldn't get to see Charlie. He'd taken Myla somewhere earlier this afternoon and wasn't back yet.

"Remember, you can come back whenever you want." Lailah's hand was on Jojo's shoulder as they watched David load up the car.

"Anytime you need anything at all, just call," Barkley chimed in, his hand over Lailah's.

Jojo felt a flood of sadness overtake her. She was so confused. One half of her brain couldn't wait to be back with Fred and Bradley. She hoped their apartment in Greenland had a couch as comfy as their beat-up Crate and Barrel pullout in Sacramento. She pictured the three of them curled up on movie night, watching a so-bad-it's-good campy horror movie. (Provided they had Netflix, or at least Blockbuster, in Nuuk.) She longed for her dads' familiar hugs and bad jokes—even for an apartment that was five degrees too cold because they refused to blast the heat.

But the other half of her brain wanted to cling to

Barkley and Lailah for dear life. These were her parents too. She'd finally had a mom who took her shopping, and told her she looked pretty, and smoothed her hair with long, graceful fingers. And Barkley's hugs felt like they could protect her from anything—maybe even her own stupid decisions. And she was leaving them behind, after only a week, just when she was getting to know them.

She turned her teary face toward her mom and dad, clutching them both in another hug. Mahalo threw his wiry arms around her waist, Bobby grabbed her side, and Nelson her right knee. Adjani and Indigo wobbled across the grass on their chubby little legs and threw their arms around her left knee. Jojo felt like she might topple over, but the family hug felt good. Maybe she could come live here again. Someday, anyway. When she was thirty and Barnsley Toole was nothing more than a snapshot in *People*'s Where Are They Now? issue.

But right now, she had to catch her United Airlines flight to Nova Scotia. She had a connecting flight in Halifax to Nuuk. She'd brought copies of two books she couldn't wait to read, *Good Omens* and *Salem's Lot*, or maybe she'd just sleep for the entire fourteen-hour flight. She was a little sad she wouldn't see Myla before she left.

"We love you," Barkley said, his voice catching in his throat. He kissed her forehead, loosening his grip and letting her go.

"'Bye, Jojo," Mahalo said. "Don't stay gone." He let go of Jojo's waist, and the other kids followed suit.

Lailah pulled out of the hug, taking Jojo's face in her graceful hands. "We'll miss you so much, Josephine," she said, a tear following the path of her graceful cheekbone. "We love you so much."

"I love you too," Jojo sobbed, folding her parents in a hug one last time as David opened the town car door. She got inside, watching her parents and the kids retreat to the stone steps of the palacelike house.

She looked at the castle, the color of lemon meringue in the dimming evening sunlight. She found the window to her room—with its white satin drapes—on the second floor. Maybe it would be waiting for her if she ever came back.

"Goodbye," she whispered to the house, the rose garden, and her family, waving to her from the front porch. David began to reverse in the long driveway, suddenly stopping.

Jojo looked into the rearview mirror. Charlie had just pulled the SUV in behind them, and Myla extracted herself from the vehicle's back seat. She looked like an angel, in a wispy white sundress and pearl-colored flats, the sparkly white Rittenhouse bag on her arm.

She strode, all business, up to the window of the town car and knocked impatiently.

"Open up," she demanded.

Jojo rolled down the window.

"Where the hell are you going?" Myla pulled her white sunglasses off, dropping them in the bag. Her green eyes glimmered.

Jojo gritted her teeth. Had Myla snapped back to über-bitch on her last day here? "Um, to Greenland, to go live with my real family. Remember?"

Myla folded her arms over her slim chest. "Yeah, but

I thought that was a self-pity thing. Or like how people say, 'I'll never drink again.'"

Jojo shook her head. "Nope, I'm outta here."

Myla opened the door. She surveyed Jojo's nails, her Dutch Tulip Red chipped from packing. She rolled her eyes. "Shut the hell up," she said, yanking Jojo by the arm. "The only place you're going is to Elle, for a decent manicure. Do I have to teach you everything?"

Once upon a time on the Upper East Side of New York City, two beautiful girls fell in love with one perfect boy. . . .

Turn the page for a peek of the *New York Times* bestselling novel by Cecily von Ziegesar

it had to be you
the gossip girl prequel

and find out how it all began.

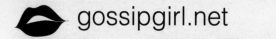 gossipgirl.net

Disclaimer: All the real names of places, people, and events have been altered or abbreviated to protect the innocent. Namely, me.

hey people!

Ever have that totally freakish feeling that someone is listening in on your conversations, spying on you and your friends while you sip lattes on the ivory-colored steps of the Metropolitan Museum of Art, following you to premieres and parties, and just generally stalking you? Well, they are. Or actually, I am. And the truth is, I've been here all along, because I'm one of you. One of the Chosen Ones.

Don't get out much? Hair so processed it's fried your brain? Perhaps you're not one of us after all and you have no clue what I'm talking about or who "we" are. Allow me to expound. We're an exclusive group of indescribably beautiful people who happen to live in those majestic, green-awninged, white-glove-doorman buildings near Central Park. We attend Manhattan's most elite single-sex private schools. Our families own yachts, estates, and vineyards in various exotic locations through-out the world. We frequent all the best beaches and the most exclusive ski resorts in Austria and Utah. We're seated immediately at the finest restaurants in the chicest neighborhoods with nary a reservation. We turn heads. But don't confuse us with Hollywood actors or models or rock stars—those people you feel like you know because you read so much about them in the tabloids, but who are actually completely boring compared to the roles they play or the ballads they sing. There's nothing boring about me or my friends, and the more I tell you about us, the more you'll be dying to know. I've kept quiet until now, but something has happened, and if I don't share it with the world I'm absolutely going to burst.

the greatest story ever told

We learned in our eleventh-grade creative writing class this week that most great stories begin in one of the following fashions: someone mysteriously disappears, or a stranger comes to town. The tale I'm about to tell is of the "someone mysteriously disappears" variety.

To be specific, **S** is gone. The steps of the Met are no longer graced with her blond splendor. We are no longer distracted in Latin class by the sight of her twirling her pale locks around and around her long, slim fingers while she daydreams about a certain emerald-eyed boy.

But keep your panties on, I'll get to that in a moment.

The point is, **S** has disappeared. And in order to solve the mystery of why she's left and where she's gone, I'm going to have to backtrack to last winter—the winter of our sophomore year—when the La Mer skin cream hit the fan and our pretty pink rose-scented bubble burst. It all began with three inseparable, perfectly innocent, über-gorgeous fifteen-year-olds. Well, they're sixteen now, and let's just say that two of them are not that innocent.

An epic such as this requires an observant, quick-witted scribe. That would be me, since I *was* at the scene of every crime, and I happen to have an impeccable eye for the most outrageous details. So sit back while I unravel the past and reveal everyone's secrets, because I know everything, and what I don't know I'll invent elaborately.

Admit it, you're already falling for me.

You know I love you,

gossip girl

like most juicy stories, it started with one boy and two girls

"Truce!" Serena van der Woodsen screamed as Nate Archibald body-checked her into a three-foot-high drift of powdery white snow. Cold and wet, it tunneled into her ears and down her pants. Nate dove on top of her, all five foot eleven inches of his perfect, golden-brown-haired, glittering-green-eyed, fifteen-year-old boyness. He smelled like Downy and the L'Occitane sandalwood soap the maid stocked his bathroom with. Serena just lay there, trying to breathe with him on top of her. "My scalp is cold," she pleaded, getting a mouthful of Nate's snow-dampened, godlike curls as she spoke.

Nate sighed reluctantly, as if he could have spent the rest of the morning outside in the frigid February meat locker that was the back garden of his family's Eighty-second-Street-just-off-Park-Avenue Manhattan town house. He rolled onto his back and wriggled like Serena's long-dead golden retriever, Guppy, when she used to let him loose on the green grass of the Great Lawn in Central Park. Then he stood up, awkwardly dusting off the seat of his neatly pressed Brooks Brothers khakis. It was Saturday, but he still wore the same clothes he wore every weekday as a sophomore at the St. Jude's School for Boys over on East End Avenue. It was the unofficial Prince of the Upper East Side uniform, the same uniform he and his classmates had been wearing since they'd started nursery school together at Park Avenue Presbyterian.

Nate held out his hand to help Serena to her feet. Behind him rose the clean-looking limestone prewar luxury buildings of Park Avenue's Golden Mile, with their terraced penthouses and plate-glass windows. Still, nothing beat living in an actual house with an entire wing of one's own and a back garden with a fountain and cherry trees in it, within walking distance of one's best friends' houses, Serendipity 3, and Barneys. Serena frowned cautiously up at Nate, worried that he was only faking her out and was about to tackle her again. "I really am cold," she insisted.

He flapped his hand at her impatiently. "I know. Come on."

She pretended to pick her nose and then grabbed his hand with her faux-snotty one. "Thanks, pal." She staggered to her feet. "You're a real chum."

Nate led the way inside. The backs of his pant legs were damp and she could see the outline of his tighty-whiteys. Really, how gay of him! He held the glass-paned French doors open and stood aside to let her pass. Serena kicked off her baby blue Uggs and scuffed her bare, Urban Decay Piggy Bank Pink–toenailed feet down the long hall to the stately town house's enormous, barely used all-white Italian Modern kitchen. Nate's father, Captain Archibald, was a former sea captain–turned-banker, and his mother was a French society hostess. They were basically never home, and when they were home, they were at the opera.

"Are you hungry?" Nate asked, following her across the gleaming white marble floor. "I'm so sick of takeout. My parents have been in Venezuela or Santa Domingo or wherever for like two weeks, and I've been eating pizza or sushi every freaking night. I asked Regina to buy ham, Swiss, Pepperidge Farm white bread, Grammy Smith apples, and peanut butter. All I want is the food I ate in kindergarten." He tugged anxiously on a messy lock of wavy golden brown hair. "Maybe I'm going through some sort of midlife crisis or something."

Like his life is so stressful?

"It's *Granny* Smith, silly," Serena informed him fondly. She opened a glossy white cupboard and found an unopened box of cinnamon-and-brown-sugar Pop-Tarts. Ripping it open, she removed one of the packets from inside, tore it open with her neat, white teeth, and pulled out a thickly frosted pastry. She sucked on the Pop-Tart's sweet, crumbly corner and hopped up on the counter, kicking the cupboards below with her size eight-and-a-half feet. Pop-Tarts at Nate's. She'd been having them there since she was five years old. And now . . . and now . . .

"Mom and Dad want me to go to boarding school next year," she announced, her enormous, almost navy blue eyes growing huge and glassy as they welled up with unexpected tears. Go away to boarding school and leave Nate? It hurt too much even to even think about.

Nate flinched as if he'd been slapped in the face by an invisible hand. He grabbed the other Pop-Tart from the packet and hopped up on the counter next to her. "No way," he responded decisively. She couldn't leave. He wouldn't allow it.

"They want to travel more," she explained, the pink, perfect curve of her lower lip trembling dangerously. "If I'm home, they feel like they need to be home more. Like I want them around? Anyway, they've arranged for me to meet some of the deans of admissions and stuff. It's like I have no choice."

Nate scooted over a few inches and wrapped his arm around her sharply defined shoulders. "The city is going to suck if you're not here," he told her earnestly. "You can't go."

Serena took a deep, shuddering breath and rested her pale blond head on his shoulder. "I love you," she murmured without thinking. Their bodies were so close the entire Nate-side of her hummed. If she turned her head and tilted her chin just so, she could have easily kissed his warm, lovely neck. And she wanted to. She was actually dying to, because she really did love him, with all her heart.

She did? Hello? Since when?!

Maybe since ballroom-dancing school way back in fourth grade. She was tall for her age, and Nate was always such a gentleman about her lack of rhythm and the way she stepped on his insteps and jutted her bony elbows into his sides. He'd finesse it by grabbing her hand and spinning her around so that the skirt of her puffy oyster-colored satin tea-length Bonpoint dress twirled out magnificently. Their teacher, Mrs. Jaffe, who had long blue hair that she kept in place with a pearl-adorned black hairnet, worshipped Nate. So did Serena's best friend, Blair Waldorf. And so did Serena—she just hadn't realized it until now. She shivered and her perfect, still-tan-from-Christmas-in-the-Caribbean skin broke out in a rash of goosebumps. Her whole body seemed to be having an adverse reaction to the idea of revealing something she'd kept so well hidden for so long, even from herself.

Nate slipped his lacrosse-toned arms around her long, narrow waist and pulled her close, tucking her pale gold head into the crook of his neck and massaging the ruts between the ribs on her back with his fingertips. The best thing about Serena was her total lack of embarrassing flab. Her entire body was as long and lean and taut as the strings on his Prince titanium tennis racket.

It was painful having such a ridiculously hot best friend. Why couldn't his best friend be some lard-assed dude with zits and dandruff? Instead he had Serena and Blair Waldorf, hands down the two hottest girls on the Upper East Side, and maybe all of Manhattan, or even the whole world.

Serena was an absolute goddess—every guy Nate knew talked about her—but she was perplexingly unpredictable. She'd laugh for hours if she spotted a cloud shaped like a toilet seat or something equally ridiculous, and the next moment she'd be wistful and sad. It was impossible to tell what she was thinking most of the time. Sometimes Nate wondered if she would've been more comfortable in a body that was slightly less perfect, because it would've given her more *incentive*, to use an SAT vocabulary word. Like she wasn't sure what she had to *aspire* to, since she basically had everything a girl could possibly want.

Blair was petite, with a pretty, foxlike face, cobalt blue eyes, and wavy chestnut-colored hair. Way back in fifth grade, Serena had told Nate she was convinced Blair had a crush on him. He started to notice that Blair did sort of stick her chest out when she knew he was looking, and she was always either bossing him around or fixing his hair. Of course Blair never admitted that she liked him, which made him like her even more.

Nate sighed deeply. No one understood how difficult it was to be best friends with two such beautiful, impossible girls.

Like he would have been friends with them if they were awkward and butt-ugly?

He closed his eyes and breathed in the sweet scent of Serena's Frédéric Fekkai Apple Cider clarifying shampoo. He'd kissed a few girls and had even gone to third base last June with L'Wren Knowes, a very experienced older Seaton Arms School senior who really did seem to know everything. But kissing Serena would be . . . different. He loved her. It was as simple as that. She was his best friend, and he loved her.

And if you can't kiss your best friend, who *can* you kiss?

Before **Vanessa** filmed her first movie,
Dan wrote his first poem,
and **Jenny** bought her first bra.

Before **Blair** watched her first Audrey Hepburn movie,
Serena left for boarding school,
and before **Nate** came between them. . . .

it had to be you
the gossip girl prequel

Available now in paperback

Spotted back in NYC:
Blair, **S**erena,
Nate, and **C**huck

And guess who will be there to
whisper all their juicy secrets?

i will always love you
a gossip girl
novel

An all-new special hardcover edition,
featuring the original cast.
Coming November 2009.

poppy
www.pickapoppy.com